Where We Begin Again

Adela Tobin

Published by Adela Tobin, 2025.

WHERE WE BEGIN AGAIN

First edition. February 28, 2025.

ISBN: 978-1764016506

Written by Adela Tobin.

For my sister, Temi. May your memory forever shine bright. And for Ella, my constant inspiration.

"We are all haunted houses. Each of us filled with rooms we have locked, versions of ourselves we have left behind, and echoes of who we once were." — Unknown

Prologue

November 2011

The sun rose early, bathing the coastal town of Inverloch in a kaleidoscope of soft pinks and golden hues. The ocean shimmered like liquid glass, its surface catching the dawn light and scattering it across the shore.

A faint breeze carried the salty tang of the sea, mingling with the sweet aroma of blooming frangipanis. It was the kind of day that seemed tailor-made for adventure—or so his father believed.

"Come on, we're not wasting a day like this!" his father declared, his booming voice filled with unyielding authority. It wasn't a suggestion; it was a decree. Resisting had never worked before, and it wouldn't now.

He hesitated momentarily, caught between obligation and his own simmering unease. All he wanted was a quiet day to himself, a chance to process the difficult conversation with his girlfriend that still lingered, unresolved.

A decision loomed between them, one that would upend everything. The clear blue skies mocked him; they felt too perfect, too calm, masking a heaviness in the air that he couldn't shake.

"I don't think I'll come along," she had said earlier, her tone clipped, her expression clouded. "I didn't sleep well. I just need some rest."

"You sure? Fresh air might do you good," he replied, though his heart wasn't in it. He knew where this conversation was heading.

"I'm not in the mood for the beach." She shook her head firmly and shrugged. Then, her voice sharpened. "Besides, we need to stop pretending. It's time to tell them. We can't keep avoiding it."

The words hit him like a punch to the gut. He nodded but said nothing, retreating into silence. She sighed, turned away, and shut the bedroom door behind her.

Downstairs, he delivered her excuse. "She's got a headache," he muttered.

His parents exchanged a glance—a fleeting look of disapproval that carried the weight of a thousand unsaid words. Sometimes, he thought their silence was worse than their criticism.

It transported him back to his childhood, to those strained meals where his father's disappointment hung over the dining table like a storm cloud. He'd never been good enough—at fly fishing, fixing things, and being the son his father wanted. And even now, as an adult, that shadow loomed large.

"Righto. I guess we'll take one car in that case," his father grumbled, his tone thick with annoyance.

As always, his mum took cues from his father's shifting moods, mirroring his reactions. It was sometimes hard to read what she actually thought about situations. It felt like she simply parroted what his dad said.

The drive to the beach was filled with an uneasy quiet, broken only by the sounds of life outside the car. The town was coming alive, bustling with summer energy.

Children darted barefoot across the sand, their laughter ringing out over the gentle roar of the waves. Teenagers sprawled lazily on towels, soaking in the sun, while surfers paddled out, waiting for the perfect wave. Pelicans soared overhead, their wings cutting graceful arcs through the sky.

But none of it registered. His mind was elsewhere, replaying the moment he had met her. It had been about three years ago, on a cherry farm in New South Wales, a sprawling property nestled between rolling hills and framed by the muted blue haze of distant mountains. Rows upon rows of cherry trees stretched as far as the eye could see, their branches heavy with ripe, glistening fruit.

The air buzzed with the sounds of cicadas, and the occasional laughter or chatter of workers spread across the orchard. The scent of sun-warmed cherries mingled with the earthy aroma of soil and crushed grass underfoot.

She'd stood out that day, not just for her straw hat, which was slightly frayed at the edges. It was how she carried herself; a lightness, an energy that seemed to ripple out and brighten everything around her. He could still see her leaning against one of the ladders, a wooden crate at her feet brimming with cherries.

"I'd kill for a cold cider right now," she said, her voice carrying above the rustling leaves as she tipped her head back toward the sky. She waved a hand in front of her face, fanning herself dramatically. "Or anything cold, really."

He had been a few rows over, sweat dripping from his own brow as he filled his bucket, but her voice drew him in, clear and lilting, filled with a mix of exasperation and humour. Before he could think better of it, he crossed over.

"I've got some water," he offered, holding out his dented canteen. "It's not cold, but you're welcome to it."

She turned to him, startled at first, then smiled a wide, genuine grin that made her brown eyes crinkle at the corners. "Ah, thanks, but I think I'll survive. Though I can't promise I won't whinge about it."

He laughed, a little surprised at his own boldness and at how easily she drew a response from him. "Well, if you pass out, we'll just blame the heat," he teased, shifting the bucket in his hand.

She pretended to consider this, her nose wrinkling in mock frustration. "Heat or cider... I guess either way, I'd be useless for the rest of the day." Her laughter rang out, clear and melodic, harmonizing with the rhythmic thuds of cherries landing in buckets around them.

They lingered there for a moment longer, exchanging stories between the rows of trees. She told him she was on a working holiday visa, chasing experiences and filling her passport with stamps. She spoke of nights spent in hostels, long bus rides through unfamiliar landscapes, and the thrill of meeting people she might never see again.

By the end of the day, as the sun dipped low and painted the orchard in colourful hues, he had worked up the nerve to ask her out for that longed-for cider.

"You mentioned cider earlier," he said, scratching the back of his neck. "What if I told you I know a place that serves the coldest cider you've ever had?"

She raised an eyebrow, pretending to deliberate. "That depends—does this place also serve chips?"

"Absolutely. Best chips in town," he replied, his grin widening.

"Well then, how could I say no?" she said, her smile softening as she tucked a loose strand of hair behind her ear.

That laugh, that smile—so easy, so genuine—had disarmed him completely.

Two weeks after their first date, they celebrated her twenty-first birthday with some of the friends they'd made working at the farm. The sun was setting as they gathered around a makeshift table draped with a picnic cloth laden with food and drinks.

"I didn't know what to get you, so I hope this isn't me stepping out of line," he said nervously, handing her a small, neatly wrapped package. Inside was an insulated water bottle, its surface adorned with a beautiful floral design, vibrant yet understated—just like her.

She laughed when she unwrapped it, her eyes lighting up as she held it up for everyone to see. "Stepping out of line? This is perfect," she said with a wink, her tone playful but warm. The others cheered and teased, but she leaned in and whispered, just loud enough for him to hear, "Now I really have no excuse to pass out from heatstroke."

From that moment on, they were inseparable. They travelled together, worked side by side in orchards and vineyards, and built a life that felt boundless and free.

The nights were their favourite—endless hours spent under the stars, talking until their voices grew hoarse, sharing secrets they hadn't dared voice to anyone else. In those moments, the world felt vast but conquerable, and they felt like they belonged to it—and to each other.

It had all seemed perfect—until his father's illness had pulled him back home, tethering him to a world of responsibilities he thought he'd left behind.

A shout jolted him from his thoughts.

He blinked, suddenly brought back to the present and aware of the commotion on the beach. People were running toward the water, their faces tight with worry. His mother's scream sliced through the air; A sound so raw, so filled with anguish, it made his blood run cold.

Heart pounding, he sprinted toward the chaos. A small crowd had gathered at the water's edge, some standing frozen, others frantically making calls. A few brave souls were already in the surf, battling the waves.

The scene was a blur—faces contorted in fear, voices shouting over the roar of the ocean.

He pushed through the crowd, his chest tightening with dread. The ominous feeling from earlier that morning crystallized into cold, hard reality. Something terrible had happened.

And in that moment, he knew. This wasn't just a ripple in the fabric of their day. This was a break, a rupture. A moment that would change everything. Forever.

Part One: Lola, Brett, and Hannah

Chapter One: Lola

Lola's gaze flickered to the television, where a detective's tense pursuit of a suspect unfolded. The music swelled, tightening the moment. She let herself sink into the scene for a second, grasping at the distraction like a lifeline.

She habitually did this—turning to something trivial whenever the weight of reality felt too heavy to bear. When a problem loomed too large, she found solace in the insignificant.

She had done it countless times, especially during the more gruelling stretches of her PhD, when her mind refused to settle on the work before her.

But just as quickly as she let herself escape, Ona's voice—sharper now—cut through the haze, pulling her back to the present.

"Lola? Were you listening at all?"

You're doing it again, aren't you? Watching another show while talking to me. Urgh. The last time, it was *Doctor Who*."

"I'm here," Lola replied, but her tone lacked conviction. "What's wrong with *Doctor Who*, anyway? You used to love that show when we were younger!"

"Yep, nothing wrong with it, but not when you're using it to deflect. So, as much as I want to talk about *Daleks* and *Weeping Angels* with you, I think the more pressing thing to discuss is what you intend to do", Ona said.

"Maybe that's what I need, though. A TARDIS – a time travel machine to take me back to simpler times. Happier times. Or fast forward me to another place and time entirely," Lola said rather distractedly. But Ona just gave a heavy sigh in response.

"I just... I don't know, Ona. I have not yet fully figured it out."

Ona sighed. Her concern for her friend now etched even more deeply into her features. Before she could respond, her phone buzzed. Her expression changed to one of mild irritation as she glanced down.

"Sorry, Lola, I have to take this. It's a client." She hesitated, her voice softening. "But promise me you'll think this through, okay? Don't make any hasty decisions. Leave me a voice note if you need to talk more. Love you!" She smiled faintly, blowing an air kiss before ending the video call.

The phone screen went dark, leaving Lola alone in the quiet hum of her living room. She stared at her phone, its last search result glaring back at her: *"**Making decisions about unplanned pregnancies.**"*

···——— ⚜ ———···

Her chest tightened. Even though she hadn't taken a pregnancy test, all the signs were evident. Three weeks earlier, she was suddenly overcome by nausea and an almost unreal increase in her sense of smell.

Just that morning, on the train, she'd nearly gagged at the smell of bacon from a nearby passenger's sandwich. Not that she disliked bacon, but the intensity of the smell, sharp and overwhelming, had turned her stomach.

Looking toward the bathroom, her eyes landed on the unopened pregnancy test sitting on the counter, a challenge she was not prepared to confront.

She really wished she could talk to someone about it. Someone in closer proximity than Ona, who was thousands of miles away. She was a childhood friend and someone she trusted to talk to about everything. It was hard to find someone like that nowadays. In many ways, Ona was the only real friend Lola had left.

Over time, friendships had faded for various reasons—some due to relocation, others because Lola hesitated to invest the effort needed to maintain them. It was a hard truth to admit, but Lola knew she was often flaky.

She'd long blamed it on her introverted nature, convincing herself she was not built for the emotional demands of close relationships. But deep down, she understood that part of her simply didn't want to try.

Maintaining new friendships felt like a chore, an endless uphill climb she didn't have the energy to face.

The people she knew now—if she was honest—weren't really friends. They were more than familiar faces but less than friends. They exchanged polite conversation, carefully avoiding deeper topics. It was easier that way, avoiding anything too personal, keeping her vulnerability locked away.

Real friends, however, were different. Real friends were rare, the kind of people she could confide in about the tangled mess of her life. The kind she could be her unfiltered, imperfect self with, without fear of judgment or abandonment.

She longed to confide in someone, but finding the opportune moment proved difficult with Ona who lived in the U.S., balancing a demanding career as an attorney with the chaos of raising two energetic boys.

Despite the distance and their busy lives, she remained Lola's oldest and dearest friend. Their bond stretched back decades to when they were just two little girls in Nigeria, neighbours and confidantes.

Ona's family moved to Lola's neighbourhood when they were both kids, and the two girls instantly hit it off. Ona had enrolled in the same primary school as Lola, and from then on, they were inseparable.

Both were only children, and they found in each other the siblings neither of them had. Their parents had breathed a quiet sigh of relief, grateful that the girls had each other to lean on, easing their guilt over the loneliness their daughters might have felt.

Their days were filled with sleepover ideas, whispered secrets, and big, fantastical plans for the future. "*She is my best friend in the whole wide world*!" they had both declared to their parents.

So, when Ona's family eventually moved away, they vowed to keep in touch. And against the odds, they had.

Through time and distance, their bond endured, a testament to the strength of their childhood connection. Ona was more than a friend; she was a lifeline to a version of Lola that felt simpler, braver, and unburdened by the complexities of adulthood.

Lola thought of the Facebook group she'd joined recently—a community for women who had relocated to Australia—just like her. At the time, it appeared to be a promising way to forge new bonds and discover a sense of community.

The group was a lively mix of women from all over the world, ranging in age and background, navigating the complexities of building a life in another country.

But it hadn't worked out the way she'd hoped.

She'd tried to engage, commenting here and there, but the conversations always seemed to dry up when she entered them, or worse, she'd get that awkward, almost hesitant response, as if people weren't quite sure how to respond to her.

She couldn't shake the feeling that some of the women regarded her a little strangely, like there was something they just didn't like about her. It wasn't the first time she'd felt that way.

Throughout her life, there had been fleeting moments where she'd catch someone staring at her, their expression unreadable, a flicker of something unreadable in their eyes.

Was it something she said? Or the way she said it? Was she socially awkward? She could never be sure.

"They make it seem like I have two heads!" Lola had said to Ona during one of their phone conversations.

"Ah, don't mind them! You're awesome - even with your two heads!" She had joked, laughing.

Lola's difficulty in putting herself out there was apparent. She'd muted the group chat weeks ago, overwhelmed by the constant stream of messages and invitations to meetups.

She'd even considered attending one of the events—a casual brunch at a nearby café—but had talked herself out of it after trying on five different outfits and hating them all.

The thought of walking into a room full of strangers, of having to make small talk and smile through her nerves, had been too much. And even if she managed to show up, what if she said something that made the women give her that *look*?

Instead, she'd spent the day on her couch, watching reruns of an old sitcom and sipping wine, convincing herself she preferred it that way. She spent most of her time by herself—or with Brett. Her world consisted mainly of him. And now, she couldn't even bring herself to face him.

With only her thoughts and an unopened pregnancy test, she was now alone, with no one to confide in. She couldn't even bring herself to do the one thing that might give her clarity.

Her phone buzzed again, shattering the silence. For a fleeting moment, she hoped it was Ona calling back to finish their conversation. But as she glanced at the screen, her heart sank. It was *him*—the one person who deserved answers she still didn't have.

Her fingers tightened around the silver chain he had given her not so long ago, the cool metal pressing into her palm as uncertainty settled in her chest.

With a heavy sigh, Lola powered down her phone, its screen fading to black. For now, she needed the silence—the absence of pressure, the space to think.

She knew she couldn't avoid it forever, even though the weight of the unanswered question loomed large - *what was she going to do?*

Chapter Two: Road Trips and Rose-Tinted Glasses (2009)

The highway stretched endlessly ahead as Brett adjusted the volume on the stereo.

The crisp autumn air drifted through the half-open windows, laced with the scent of eucalyptus and sun-warmed earth.

A faint haze still clung to the horizon—a lingering reminder of the fires that had ravaged Victoria just weeks earlier. **Black Saturday,** they were calling it. The news was still replaying footage of scorched landscapes and smouldering townships, the kind of devastation that didn't just fade into the past.

"All those families displaced..." Hannah murmured, gazing out the window. "I can't imagine the sheer terror of it all."

Brett shook his head slowly and said, "Yeah. It's just so bloody awful." He tightened his grip on the steering wheel, his gaze steady on the road ahead. A heavy silence settled between them, the weight of the tragedy pressing down on the moment.

Then, slowly, the tension began to ease. The sun dipped lower in the sky, casting long golden streaks across the dashboard. A soft breeze drifted in through the open window, carrying with it the scent of eucalyptus and warm earth.

Hannah propped her feet up on the dash, her bare toes tapping absently to the rhythm of Delta Goodrem's *Innocent Eyes* playing through the speakers. She tilted her head back, letting the wind tousle her thick, curly hair, the corners of her lips curving into a smile.

"I can't believe we're actually doing this," she said, a quiet thrill in her voice.

Brett grinned, casting her a sideways glance from the driver's seat. His dark blue eyes gleamed with mischief, the corners crinkling just slightly as he flashed that easy, boyish smile of his. The late afternoon sunlight caught in his wavy, sandy brown hair, deepening the hint of red that always seemed to burn through in the right light.

"What, running away from responsibility for a few days? Skipping work shifts and missing that group project meeting?" His fingers drummed lightly against the steering wheel. "Sounds like the perfect plan to me."

She laughed, shaking her head. "I meant more that we finally have the chance to just... go. No schedules, no deadlines, no expectations. Just us, the road, and whatever town we end up in next."

Not that she could ignore her studies forever. Distance education made things easier—she could work from anywhere, as long as she had her laptop and enough patience to sit through recorded lectures—but that didn't mean she wasn't falling behind. She'd promised herself she'd catch up when they got back.

They had already spent the past couple of weeks in Adelaide, bouncing between cheap motels and crashing with backpackers they'd met along the way. Now, they were restless again, itching for open roads and unfamiliar places.

"Where exactly are we heading?" Brett asked, stretching his arms as he drove.

Hannah shrugged. "Somewhere along the coast. Maybe Yorke Peninsula? Or we could go further west—Eyre Peninsula, see the cliffs and the beaches."

"Or we could just drive until we hit something interesting," Brett said with a grin.

"Exactly," she said, turning to him, her beautiful brown eyes gleaming with excitement.

He shook his head, a smile playing on his lips. "Alright, mystery it is!"

With that, they continued forward, the road unfurling ahead of them like an unwritten story.

Chapter Three: Chichester, 2016

Hannah stood before the canvas; her steely gaze fixed on the image she had sketched. Frustration growing with each passing second, she meticulously examined every line and curve for what felt like an eternity. This wasn't the vision she had imagined. The powerful image in her mind had become a lacklustre version on the canvas.

She shook her head, letting out an irritated grunt as she clenched her jaw. She grabbed a large mop brush and dipped it into thick, inky black paint. With a single, deliberate stroke, she slashed across her work, obliterating it. The act was both cathartic and disheartening. Hours of effort were erased in moments, but she didn't care.

Something was wrong—something she couldn't quite name, but it poisoned everything she touched.

With a sharp clink against the table, she set the brush down, grimacing. Lately, she felt off-kilter, as if she were walking through life on uneven ground.

She had always been a perfectionist, but this was different. This was a deeper malaise, one that gnawed at her creativity and sapped her energy. It had to stop. She needed to clear her head.

Deciding on a change of scenery, she moved away from her easel. Fresh air might help. And coffee—*always coffee*. She would head to the café on the high street and take a brisk walk along the canal.

The idea of sitting on a bench by the water, letting her thoughts drift, seemed like the balm her mind needed. Perhaps a book would provide better company than her tangled thoughts.

Crossing the room, she picked up a novel she'd been trying—and failing—to immerse herself in for weeks.

Instinctively, she reached for her dog's leash upon stepping into the hallway. "*Coco?*" she called out before the realization hit her like a wave. He wasn't there. He wouldn't ever be there again.

Her hand froze mid-air, and she smiled ruefully at the reflex. The void that Coco left behind felt just as raw even after months had passed. He had been her loyal companion for a few years, his joyful presence a constant source of comfort.

Losing him to a heart disease had been devastating. Though she threw herself into her work to cope, some days were more challenging than others.

Her phone buzzed in her pocket, snapping her out of her thoughts. She glanced at the screen: a message from her mum. Without reading it, she shoved the phone back into her pocket.

She didn't need to read it to know the tone. It would be yet another complaint about her inattention, and another list of grievances about the world's injustices would follow.

Her mum had a talent for playing the victim, a skill honed over decades. Despite alienating most people in her life, she had managed to surround herself with enablers who indulged her endless pity parties.

Hannah's mind wandered back to the last time they had met. It was as brief a lunch as she could have afforded. Once again, her mother centred the conversation on her disappointments and hurt feelings.

Her mum had been scrolling through photos of her ex-husband and his new wife on social media, her sharp-tongued commentary punctuated by sips of Chardonnay.

It felt like her mum always needed a drink whenever she met with her. She knew her mum still held some resentment about the past. They both did, and meeting up usually felt contrived and stress-inducing.

"What could he possibly see in her?" she had said, thrusting the phone toward Hannah. The photo showed her dad and his partner on a bridge in Venice, holding hands and looking happy and radiant.

Her dad's partner, Martha, in her wide-brimmed straw hat and gold-striped kaftan dress, was the antithesis of her mother's meticulously styled appearance. Her dad's posture displayed a newfound ease, his smile exuding a warmth unseen by Hannah for a long time.

"It's not all about looks, Mum," Hannah had said, her tone tinged with exasperation. Although what she wanted to say was far harsher, the words remained trapped in her throat. Her mother's vanity and bitterness had always been a barrier between them, a wall built brick by brick over the years.

With disdain dripping from her words, her mother had continued. "I truly don't understand the appeal here. What could he possibly see in her? Look at all that grey hair!" she said, scrolling through more photos.

"Just look at what she's wearing in this photo. Zero dress sense or sophistication. She always manages to look dowdy in every photo."

"Why? Because it's not a branded wear?" Hannah asked, eliciting a sharp look of disapproval from her mum.

Hannah recalled her mum's immense pride in her appearance. Abi, her mum, was still a beautiful woman. Her fair skin remained smooth and taut. Her thick, full-bodied honey blond hair was styled neatly in a chic bob, and even in her mid-sixties, she maintained a slim physique.

Abi would joke to friends who complimented her that her daughter, Hannah, should be grateful for her inherited genes. "I even considered adopting or surrogacy instead of wrecking my figure with pregnancy," Abi would say with a laugh, leaving Hannah wondering just how close to the truth this 'joke' was.

Hannah had felt her patience fray as her mother shoved the phone in her face. "Do you think she's attractive?" Abi asked her daughter, her voice puzzled and irritated.

"Mum, please stop," Hannah said irritably, handing the phone back to her. She wondered if her mum's disdain for Martha had less to do with her father moving on and more to do with who he had chosen.

To Hannah, it seemed her mum felt affronted by the idea of being replaced—and by someone she deemed so utterly unremarkable.

Despite being unhappy for years, her parents, her mother especially, always proudly displayed her attractive husband, relishing in her friends' envy. "She's not even his type," her mum had muttered in frustration, as though that simple fact rendered Martha's existence offensive.

Returning to the present, the crisp air's chill acted as a wake-up call as Hannah sighed and stepped outside.

The early afternoon light cast a soft glow over the cobbled streets. She tugged her coat tighter around her as she made her way to the cafe. The café's 18th-century façade concealed a labyrinth of beamed rooms and wonky doorways, leading to a charming courtyard garden brimming with flowers and cobbled paths.

Inside, the air was thick with the scent of freshly baked scones and the deep, nutty aroma of coffee. Hannah inhaled, letting the warmth of the café momentarily chase away the lingering cold.

The barista moved with effortless precision, the hiss of steaming milk and the soft clink of porcelain weaving into the low hum of conversation. The air smelled of roasted coffee and something faintly sweet—maybe vanilla or caramel.

As she waited, she absently traced patterns on the worn wooden counter, her fingers moving in lazy circles. Her thoughts, however, were anything but still—drifting, unraveling, looping back on themselves.

At last, her flat white arrived, the delicate latte art swirled on top like a quiet invitation. She wrapped her fingers around the cup and stepped back into the crisp afternoon air. The heat seeped through her gloves, warming her palms as she took her first careful sip, letting the rich, velvety coffee ground her in the moment.

The familiar path to the canal beckoned, the sound of her boots tapping softly against the pavement as she wove past slow-moving shoppers and the occasional cyclist.

The path was damp from the morning frost, and the fallen leaves along the towpath crunched softly underfoot.

She settled onto her favourite bench, a weathered wooden seat that overlooked the tranquil canal waters. The canal mirrored the overcast sky, its surface occasionally disturbed by the ripple of a passing duck or the gentle drift of a fallen leaf.

In the distance, the spire of Chichester Cathedral stood tall against the skyline. Narrowboats, their exteriors adorned with vibrant paint, were moored along the banks, some emitting the faint aroma of wood smoke from their chimneys.

The quiet was punctuated by the soft hum of distant conversations and the occasional rustle of leaves as a breeze swept through.

Hannah cradled her coffee, the steam curling into the cold air. The book she had brought remained unopened on her lap as she gazed out over the serene water, her thoughts drifting like the leaves on the canal's surface.

Her thoughts drifted, unbidden, to Coco, Chase, and the fortress of solitude she had carefully constructed around herself.

Chase had tried so hard to break through that fortress, but she'd eventually pushed him away, just as she did with everyone. He had deserved more—someone who could meet his kindness with honesty, not walls of secrets and silence.

Her phone buzzed in her pocket, jolting her from her thoughts. This time, she didn't ignore it. She hesitated upon catching sight of her mum's name on the screen. Biting the bullet, she picked up the phone. The phone rang for a few seconds before she picked up, the chilly silence of her mother filling the air.

"Hi, Mum," said Hannah, her voice steady despite her tiredness.

Abi replied, her tone dripping with wounded indignation. "So, you've finally decided to answer my call?" "I was starting to think something awful had happened to you."

Hannah tightened her grip on the phone. "Mum, you just got back from a cruise. You make it sound like you were in the ICU or something."

Her mum countered, sniffling theatrically, "I have been sick." It's been the absolute worst. There's nobody to care for me. Not a single person checking in."

Hannah's jaw clenched. I've also been coping with a lot, even though I'm sorry to hear you've been unwell. Work has been overwhelming, and, well... I lost Coco recently."

"Coco? Who's that? A friend?"

"My dog, Mum. Coco is - was my dog." Hannah said, feeling some irritation creeping into her voice. Her tone rose slightly as a couple walking by glanced at her. She lowered her gaze, a little embarrassed.

"Oh, sweetheart, that's terrible to hear. I didn't even realize you had a dog! You keep your life so... private, dear. It's a wonder I know anything about what's happening with you. I'd never have known about Chase if he hadn't picked up your phone the last time I called. He sounds like a nice fella. I checked him out on Facebook. He's good-looking, too!"

"Well, he wasn't meant to have answered my phone," Hannah replied, her voice tinged with irritation and a hint of embarrassment. In her mind, the memory of that day flickered.

...———⚜———...

She had met Chase at an art fair she often attended, a vibrant gathering of creative souls. Chase had lingered at her stall, studying her painting with an intensity that made her self-conscious yet flattered. Their conversation had begun cautiously, but his genuine interest in her work had disarmed her.

One afternoon, Fiona, an older woman that Hannah had befriended at the fairs, teased her with a knowing smile, "He might be interested in more than your paintings, Hannah." "That gentleman certainly seems smitten. I think he has gone soft on you."

"Come on, Fi! Just because a bloke appreciates your work doesn't mean he's about to declare his undying love for me. Gimme a break!" Hannah had replied, rolling her eyes playfully.

"Oh well. We'll see about that! If you don't want him, pass him on to me," Fiona had quipped cheekily, earning a hearty laugh from Hannah.

Despite her initial dismissal, she had slowly grown fond of Chase and his increasing presence in her life. He wasn't pushy, just persistent in a quiet, comforting way.

Chase would send her photos of places he visited, peppering his messages with thoughtful notes about why she might find them inspiring for her art. Before she realized it, she was looking forward to their exchanges and eventually joined him on a few of his adventures.

"Do you reckon there's more to these adventures together than just inspiration for your art?" he'd asked one evening as they shared a bottle of wine at a vineyard in Chichester. The golden shades of the sunset bathed the rolling vines in warmth, adding an air of romance to the moment.

"I do enjoy your company, Chase," she said softly, her cheeks flushing.

"I enjoy yours too. It's no secret that I have feelings for you, Hannah," He confessed with a steady yet vulnerable voice.

"I want to spend more time with you."

She replied, meeting his piercing grey eyes, "I'm truly flattered," her heart pounding in her chest.

"I sense a "but' coming on," he said with a nervous chuckle, bracing himself. She laughed nervously, too, before replying.

"I just... I'm not sure I'm ready for anything serious. I've got - baggage," she confessed, her words tumbling out in a rush. "I do, however, enjoy spending time with you. I just don't want to lead you on or keep you waiting."

His expression softening, Chase said, "I get it. To be honest, we all have baggage. I'm not here to rush you into anything. Let's just take it as it comes."

And so, they did. Their relationship blossomed in its own unhurried way, and soon, Chase introduced her to his family. That evening, his sister had pulled her aside after they'd had dinner.

"You're the first person he has brought home in a long time. I was starting to wonder if he ever would," she said, her tone warm but curious.

"Really? Why's that?" Hannah asked before quickly adding, "Not that there's anything wrong with staying single."

"It's just... his last relationship ended badly. His ex – she proposed to him—and recorded the whole thing on social media. She immediately called it off when his reaction was not as she anticipated. It was all so public and messy," his sister explained.

"I see." Hannah nodded, shifting slightly in discomfort as they delved into a personal aspect of Chase's life he hadn't shared with her before.

A sense of intrusion crept over her, accompanied by an unexpected sense of guilt. She didn't want to be the next woman to let him down. Yet, she wasn't even sure what she wanted from this relationship just yet.

Chase had been chatting with his dad in the courtyard when Hannah glanced at him. She felt a pang of sympathy for him.

Later that evening, Chase asked as he drove her home, "You're awfully quiet. Was my family that terrible?

"No, not at all. They're lovely. It's just... your sister mentioned your ex," Hannah said hesitantly. "I didn't know you were that close to getting married."

Chase sighed, gripping the steering wheel a little tighter. "Perhaps I should have told you. It feels like a lifetime ago, but yeah, it was dramatic. I wasn't ready for that kind of commitment, and it all fell apart in the worst way."

"It's okay," she said, trying to sound reassuring. "Since we've never promised each other full disclosure, my feelings about spending time with you remain unchanged."

He had smiled warmly at her when she said this.

The conversation had left Hannah with a strange mix of emotions. She feared that wanting to know more about him might lead to questions about her own past.

The incident with her phone happened shortly after dinner with his family. Chase had been over while she worked on a painting, and their comfortable rhythm allowed her to focus without distraction.

When her phone rang, she'd barely registered it until she realized he'd answered it.

"Chase, why did you pick up my phone? You didn't even know if I wanted to talk to her," she snapped after her mother's call ended.

"But - she's your mum. I thought you'd want to talk to her," he replied, his voice laced with hurt.

"It's inappropriate to make assumptions like that!" she retorted. "There are things about me that you don't understand."

Chase frowned. "Are you ashamed of me? Is that why you don't want anyone to know about us?"

"No! It's not like that," she said, frustration bubbling to the surface. "I just prefer to keep things private." She was quiet before adding, "Chase, I think you are making assumptions."

"Maybe. But I'm starting to wonder if we're on the same page about what *this* is," he said, his voice heavy with uncertainty.

Hannah fell silent. This wasn't how she had envisioned the situation would unfold. Just when she had started to feel a sense of stability, he had to disrupt the fragile balance they'd worked so hard to maintain.

That day, they downplayed the phone incident, acting as if it were insignificant. But something had shifted between them afterwards. Hannah had rebuilt her walls, thicker this time, and Chase could sense it.

He'd stuck around, hoping that patience might be the key, believing that if he gave her enough space, she'd let her guard down and trust him, at least a little. But she withdrew further, becoming increasingly distant.

The excuses came first—claims of being busy. Then, his calls went unanswered, and his messages were ignored for days.

The distance between them grew wider, but neither acknowledged it directly.

Chase continued reaching out, sending her thoughtful messages and invitations, but Hannah's responses became sporadic, lacking the warmth they once held. She convinced herself it was better this way—better to let things drift than to face the truth head-on.

One evening, after a particularly long and exhausting day at the studio, Hannah sat on her couch, staring at an unread message from Chase. *Can we talk?* It was simple, direct, and filled with the weight of everything unspoken. She hesitated before typing a reply. *I don't know if that's a good idea right now.*

The response was almost immediate. *Hannah, I don't understand what happened. If you don't want this, at least tell me. I deserve that much.*

Her fingers hovered over the keyboard, but no words came. She knew he was right. He deserved an explanation. But what could she say? That she was afraid? That she didn't trust herself to let someone in completely? That every time she let someone get close, they either left, or she found a way to push them away first? Instead of replying, she turned off her phone and buried her face in her hands.

Weeks passed, and the silence between them became absolute. She saw glimpses of him on social media—pictures from his hikes, snapshots of him at art exhibitions, a candid photo of him laughing with friends. He looked happy. He looked like he had moved on. That should have been a relief, but instead, it felt like a weight pressing down on her chest.

One late autumn afternoon, on her return home from a walk she found herself outside the café where they had once spent hours talking. The memory of his easy laughter, the way he had always reached for her hand absentmindedly, played in her mind like an old movie. She lingered outside for a moment before turning away, her footsteps quickening.

The past had a way of catching up, no matter how hard she tried to outrun it.

That evening, she pulled out an old sketchbook and flipped through its pages. Amid unfinished drawings and quick studies, she found a sketch of Chase—one she had done absentmindedly while he talked about a book he was reading. She traced the lines of his face with her fingers, the ache of what she had lost settling deep in her bones.

Taking a deep breath, she reached for her phone and typed a message. *I'm really sorry.*

She stared at the words for what felt like forever, debating whether to send them. In the end, she put the phone away without pressing *send*. Some things were better left unsaid.

She had pushed him away without so much as an explanation, leaving him in the dark and herself filled with unresolved guilt. And now, she had made the mistake of bringing it up with her mother.

Her mother's voice droned on, but Hannah's mind wandered, pulled backward into the past - to Chase.

"Hannah?" Her mother's voice cut through the haze of memory, sharp and demanding. "Are you even listening to me?"

Hannah blinked, the past dissolving as she refocused on the present conversation.

Her mum's tone on the phone shifted abruptly. "Broken up? Why? What did you say to him?"

Hannah clenched her jaw, her frustration bubbling to the surface. "Why do you automatically assume it was me?" she snapped.

Her mother sighed dramatically as if it were a practised performance. "I'm merely saying that he adored you, Hannah." Her voice carried a hint of exasperation. "You two were such a good-looking couple. You seemed happy with him."

She paused for a moment before continuing. "I saw all those photos of you two together—he always looked so smitten. Do you know how rare it is to find someone like that nowadays?"

Her tone softened, turning almost wistful. "He gave off a friendly and warm vibe when I spoke to him on the phone." Another sigh. "I just can't imagine him doing anything so terrible to warrant this.

The words were more painful than Hannah wanted to acknowledge. Her voice trembled as she bit back, "But you can picture me doing something horrible, can't you? Spoiling it all. Is that what you're saying? That this, too, is my fault?"

Her mum's response came quickly, a jab barely concealed in a veil of concern. "It's a habit of yours, you know, to *retreat*. Just the same as when you ran off to another continent and went quiet on us for what felt like an eternity. Were you running from us? From me?" Her voice faltered slightly at the end, an almost imperceptible crack, but Hannah caught it.

A knot formed in her stomach, twisting tighter with each passing second. Her nails dug into the edges as she clenched her phone tightly. "Mum, I have to go," she said abruptly, cutting her off mid-sentence. Her tone was sharp, final.

Ending the call, she lowered the phone with a trembling hand before her mum could reply. She breathed out shakily and stared out at the canal in front of her.

The water rippled softly, her distorted reflection blurring and reforming with the gentle current. It felt strangely poetic, like a mirror of her chaotic emotions—fractured, restless, and impossible to hold still.

Renewed in determination, she marched to her laptop upon returning home.

Opening her email, she clicked on a folder labelled '*Past*' and read through all the fifty-seven unread messages.

Her hands trembled as she scrolled, but she kept going. It was time to confront what happened *before*, no matter how much it hurt.

Part Two: 2024

Chapter Four: Sheena

Sheena aimed the rolled-up tea towel at the figure sprawled on her sofa, motionless, fast asleep. "Time to get up, mate," she called. For a split second, she was tempted to just scream out loud, but she quelled that thought and smiled cheekily to herself.

She'd tried everything else—clattering pans in the kitchen, nudging him lightly—but Alex could sleep through a hurricane.

She'd gotten creative in the past: turning up the heat to bake him out of bed or blasting music at full volume. Today, though, she didn't have the patience.

She had a birthday gig to attend - photographing for a thirteen-year-old party and a long list of other errands to run. On top of it all, there was a meeting later with someone mysterious.

The message had been cryptic, mentioning an engagement. It might be a potential client, though she wasn't entirely sure. Still, curiosity tugged at her, and she felt compelled to find out more about what this person wanted.

Alex groaned and stirred; his face half-buried in the pillow she'd reluctantly lent him the night before. "What time is it?" he mumbled, his voice thick with sleep, eyes barely open.

"Almost ten," Sheena replied briskly. "I need to leave soon. I've got a long list of errands and *someone* to see."

Alex, stifling a yawn and stretching languidly, drawled, "Right, okay. Any chance I can have a coffee before I head out? That sofa of yours is surprisingly comfy."

"Don't get too used to it," Sheena said, her eyes narrowing as she reached for the kettle.

Alex smirked, feigning hurt. "Harsh", he said.

"I mean it," she added, her tone sharpening. With hands on hips, she turned to face him fully. "This whole crashing-on-my-sofa thing?" She gestured toward the living room. "It has to stop."

Alex looked sheepish, running a hand over his shaved head—a look that had made her do a double-take the first time they met at a university Halloween party that seemed like a lifetime ago. Since then, a messy blend of friendship, romance, and an ambiguous state of affairs had marked their journey, leading to their present circumstances.

She had somehow become his unofficial therapist, the one he vented to about his rocky relationship with Natasha, his wife.

Alex sighed. "I just—things with Nat aren't easy. I don't know how to make them better."

"I'm sorry," Sheena said, her voice firm. "But that's something you need to figure out with her, not by hiding out here. It's inappropriate for you to crash here just because Nat's mad at you." It was his second time finding a reason to stay over at her place.

Alex sighed, rubbing his temples. "We're not doing anything bad, Sheena. We're just friends."

Folding her arms, Sheena countered, "Friends with a history. A history your partner absolutely despises—understandably."

Leaning forward, Alex rested his elbows on his knees and sighed heavily.

Sheena pressed on. "What are you even telling her when you don't go home? Is she aware that you are staying here?"

He hesitated, the flush creeping into his face giving him away before he even opened his mouth. The words tumbled like a confession as he admitted, "She was overseas the first time I stayed here. Last night, I sent her a text saying I was at my sister's place. She's not currently on talking terms with Ella, so she can't exactly call to verify."

Sheena shook her head, eyebrows raised. "Nice that you have it all figured out. So, you lie to her then. Because the last time I checked, we weren't related."

"She wouldn't understand," Alex said in a quieter voice. "You know she wouldn't. What's the point of telling her the truth?"

Sympathy and frustration warred within her as she stared at him. This wasn't her mess to untangle, yet somehow, she'd been dragged right into the middle of it.

"Gosh, Alex! Stop being such an idiot! She is your wife, and you should not be keeping secrets from her. These ridiculous fights are putting me in an awkward situation," Sheena said, grabbing milk from the fridge, her frustration evident.

"I'm okay with telling her I stayed at your place. I don't think there's anything to hide," Alex said, taking the mug of coffee from Sheena, whose arched brow and piercing stare conveyed a clear *Are you being serious right now* look?

"Wait, just to clarify, are we referring to the same Natasha?" You know, the one who hates my bloody guts?" Sheena snapped; her voice laced with sharpness she hadn't entirely meant. She set her hands on her hips, a subtle but unmistakable challenge in her stance.

"Bloody hell, Alex! If you tell her, she'll probably show up here, scratch my eyes out, and then serve you breakfast with it. Do not tell her anything about us."

The venom in her tone reflected the unspoken truth they both knew too well—there was no love lost between Sheena and Natasha.

Sheena vividly recalled the first time she'd locked eyes with Natasha at Alex's birthday party. He and Natasha had only been dating a couple of months then, and when he insisted Sheena attend, she reluctantly agreed. Natasha's icy gaze had met hers the moment she entered the room, a silent but definitive declaration of war. To Natasha, she was the enemy.

Things escalated when Natasha and Alex moved in together. Natasha had given him an ultimatum: sever ties with Sheena or end their relationship. Under pressure, and with few options, Alex gave in.

He had ghosted Sheena completely for a long time—until he finally realized she was a part of his life that he did not want to let go of.

Alex sighed heavily. "Natasha is aware that I've had close friends before her. I mean, you and I have a history that goes back much further than my relationship with her. That should count for something," he said, his voice almost pleading.

Sheena thought bitterly, *but you chose her*, her lips tightening to keep the words from escaping. A wave of annoyance and sadness coursed through her, though she kept her expression guarded.

When Alex met Natasha, it was clear to Sheena that she never stood a chance. Natasha came from wealth; her family owned the company where Alex worked.

There was an immediate and undeniable power imbalance. Alex's circle of friends, who had always viewed Sheena with polite but thinly veiled disapproval, thought Natasha was a perfect fit - refined, polished, and sophisticated. Conversely, Sheena embodied everything they looked down on - carefree and unpredictable.

Alex had once loved that about Sheena. But as he climbed the social ladder, the things that had drawn him to her began to seem like liabilities.

Sheena knew he had always dreamed of living a life of glamour, and Natasha gave him access to it.

Alex's life had taken a dramatic turn he hadn't anticipated. His first trip from Denmark to Australia was intended as a brief visit to reconnect with his estranged father. His father had moved to Australia decades ago, starting a new life with a new family, leaving a chasm of physical and emotional distance between them.

What began as a tentative visit evolved into something much more profound. His reconnection with his father proved unexpectedly rewarding; awkward silences between father and son had slowly yielded to shared stories, laughter, and understanding. He also discovered a bond with his two younger half-sisters, whose energy and warmth had surprised him.

For the first time in years, he felt a sense of belonging he hadn't realized he'd been missing.

What was intended as a temporary arrangement solidified into a permanent fixture. Alex had chosen to stay, planting roots in a once-foreign country that now felt like home.

Over the years, he worked his way into the fabric of Australian and Danish relations, re-enrolling at the University to gain a better advantage in international relations. Eventually, he secured a prestigious position as an honorary consul at the Danish High Commission.

The role offered a life beyond his wildest dreams: elegant receptions, high-profile diplomatic events, and meetings with influential dignitaries.

It was a world of polished smiles and sharp suits, speeches over clinking glasses, and handshakes that carried the weight of unspoken agreements. Yet, despite the grandeur, Alex never lost sight of why he had come to Australia in the first place: to rebuild connections with his family and himself.

That world he and Sheena had shared felt light-years away from the life he lived now. Once upon a time, their weekends had been electric—wild adventures filled with dancing, club-hopping, late-night kebabs, and spontaneous rides through the city.

They'd stayed up until dawn, watching movies, making out in the backseat of his car, and driving aimlessly with no destination in mind. It was chaotic and carefree, and for a while, it was perfect.

But then, everything shifted. As the wild weekends ended, formal galas and black-tie events began. Sheena couldn't keep up—her edges too jagged for the polished perfection Alex's new world demanded.

At first, the changes were subtle: a cancelled plan here, a vague excuse there. Then, one day, he said it outright - She needed to "grow up." Life, he told her, wasn't one "big, endless party."

His words, though long spoken, still wounded her. And when he told her he'd met someone he was serious about, the blow had already been softened by resignation. By then, she'd accepted her fate. She wasn't the woman he wanted to introduce to his inner circle or build his life with. She was the one he had found easy to keep on the sidelines, indulging in secret.

There was radio silence a couple of years after Alex had tied the proverbial knot with Natasha. Although Sheena hadn't heard from him, mutual friends informed her of the newlywed couple's activities.

She had known about the lavish wedding, the idyllic honeymoon on the Amalfi Coast, and the housewarming party they had thrown when they had moved to a bigger house in Melbourne's northern suburb.

Some of their mutual friends at university couldn't hide the glee in their voices as they shared what they knew. Some delivered it with an *"I told you so—he was never that into you,"* while others framed it as a favour, divulging details of Alex's happy life without her. Maybe they thought it would help her move on. In a way, it did.

She had already distanced herself from most of their shared connections, realizing a fresh start was what she needed. Perhaps, in the end, she was even taking some of Alex's advice—to "grow up" and finally face her demons.

But marital bliss was short-lived as Alex began to feel the strain of Natasha's family. Their involvement extended beyond business matters—they wanted to dictate the course of their lives: where they lived when they should have children, and even who they socialized with.

Alex felt he could never truly escape them, especially Natasha's mother and sisters, who were always present on weekends and holidays.

He noticed that Natasha changed when they were around—she became more conceited and more critical. She would join in when her sisters mocked what they considered gauche or unbecoming.

His Danish accent, initially charming, soon lost its appeal. Now, they ridiculed him for not pronouncing words "properly." On several occasions, Natasha's mother would ask him to repeat a word, only to feign a bemused expression and criticize him for not enunciating it the way she expected.

Alex always knew they were snobbish. From the beginning, they had treated him with mild suspicion, wary of his relationship with Natasha. But being who she was, Natasha had always gotten what she wanted.

At first, she had stood up for him. She excused his rough edges and made it clear that her family's opinions wouldn't change her mind.

Alex had hoped that, over time, he would either grow accustomed to their ways, or they would accept him into the fold, and the snide remarks would cease.

Instead, the barbs persisted. More and more, he felt their interactions were designed to remind him of his "place' and how fortunate he was to have married Natasha.

Their constant presence and judgment slowly weakened his confidence and strained their marriage. When Alex tried to discuss his feelings, Natasha dismissed his concerns. "Just ignore them, babe. You know how they are. They don't mean any harm, and you know they *love* you," she would say, brushing it off, as she did with most things she didn't care enough about.

Fate, it seemed, intervened when Alex and Sheena unexpectedly reunited years later at Rod Laver Arena during the Australian Open. What were the odds of the two of them attending the same game, alone, on the same evening?

It was one of those balmy January nights in Melbourne when the heat clung to the city long after sunset, wrapping itself around the residents like a heavy blanket. The air hummed with the faint scent of eucalyptus and the distant chatter of cicadas, the soundtrack of an Australian summer.

Natasha, who had never been a tennis fan and detested the sweltering heat even more, had waved Alex off with little more than a shrug. "Enjoy yourself," she had said, retreating into the comfort of the air conditioning as he grabbed his tickets and headed out the door.

The match was a doubles game, full of energy and precise coordination that kept the audience engaged with the occasional roar of excitement from the stands.

The crowd was sparser than Alex had expected. Perhaps Melbourne's notoriously unpredictable January weather had scared off a few would-be attendees. Still, the game had its charm—fast-paced volleys, strategic lobs, and moments of tension that made even the casual fans in the audience lean forward in their seats.

On his way to get a drink, Alex saw her in the distance, her profile recognizable even after so many years. He hesitated, unsure if it was really her. But the moment her name left his lips—tentative and soft—Sheena turned, and their eyes met.

Sheena had initially planned to attend the game with a friend, but her companion had bailed at the last minute due to work obligations. She had almost talked herself out of going, but something had nudged her forward. Seeing Alex again in such an unexpected place felt surreal.

After the match, they decided to continue the evening together and walked down to a bustling Irish pub in Richmond for dinner. The pub buzzed with lively music and the hum of conversations, the air filled with a mix of laughter, loud chatter, and the clinking of glasses. Despite the vibrant and busy atmosphere, they had managed to find a cozy corner to settle into.

The evening's warmth, the game's adrenaline, and the fortunate reunion combined to create an almost magical aura around them.

The walk to the pub had been punctuated by a faint but undeniable sense of nostalgia. Something about being in Sheena's presence again awakened an energy within him he hadn't felt in a long time.

Sheena had a rare ability to make him feel completely comfortable. Unlike many in his life—polished, pretentious, and fixated on appearances—she was effortlessly genuine. There were no false airs, just a refreshing honesty that grounded him.

Over dinner, Alex confided in her about his life since they last spoke, sharing his inner struggles with a candour he rarely allowed himself. It felt almost therapeutic, natural. But when Sheena revealed she was seeing someone, a strange sadness crept over him. There was also regret, the kind that lingered in the spaces between unspoken words.

He remained happy for her, though aware Sheena deserved far more than he could offer. But even as she spoke about her new relationship, Alex couldn't help but notice the subtle lack of enthusiasm in her voice. She described it as "going well," but there was a hollowness in her tone, a reluctance to delve deeper.

A bittersweet ache reminded him of their past and lingering bond, and he wondered if she felt it, too.

By the end of the evening, they had agreed to keep in touch. At the time, it had felt like the right decision. They were both now in committed relationships, which gave them a sense of accountability and made it easier to set boundaries. But even then, something unspoken hovered between them—a tension neither dared to acknowledge, but both silently understood.

"Do you agree?" Sheena's voice shook him out of his reverie. He looked at her blankly. "Sorry, what did you say?"

"Flipping heck, Alex! It looks like you might need a much stronger cup of coffee than I have at home." She said. "I don't think crashing at my place can happen again," she said, watching him for a sign of agreement.

He shrugged. "We are just friends, Sheena.'"

"Yes, and I want it to remain that way."

He nodded slowly. "Ok. That's what I want, too. They left it at that, looking at each other for what felt like a long while before Alex walked over to her, hugged her and leaned in to kiss her.

Chapter Five: Hello, Stranger

Lola chose a nearby café for the meetup. It was one of those eclectic places that prided itself on great coffee and an excellent brunch menu. It was cozy, with mismatched furniture, vintage armchairs beside modern wooden tables, and colourful cushions scattered about. The walls were adorned with an eclectic mix of artwork, the kind that made patrons stop mid-sip to take a closer look.

She selected a corner table by a bookshelf stacked with a curated collection of books and magazines. It was her usual spot, where she often worked on her thesis. On weekdays, the café was calm, an easy space to focus, though more often than not, she found herself staring out the window, her mind drifting elsewhere.

Today, though, she wasn't here to work. Today, the usual calm of the café wasn't enough to quieten the unease in her chest. Even the chatty barista, Cathy, failed to draw her into a conversation.

"Here's your matcha soy latte, dear," Cathy said, sliding the cup across the counter. She then tilted her head, eyes catching on Lola's earrings. "Ooh, love these. Where'd you get 'em?"

Lola's fingers brushed over the dangling pieces absentmindedly. "Ah, thanks," she murmured.

On any other day, she would've gone into a story about how she found them in a small thrift store tucked away in the city. It had been a birthday gift to herself. Intricate metal frames set with turquoise and amber stones—both modern and rustic, like something from another time.

But today, her thoughts were too tangled to hold a conversation. Instead, she gave a faint smile and said, "They were a gift."

Cathy grinned. "Rad gift," she said with a wink, turning to attend to the next customer.

Lola let out a slow breath and walked back to her corner. The café wasn't too crowded, just a few scattered patrons—a couple speaking softly in a language that sounded Eastern European, a man tapping away on his laptop.

She curled her fingers around her takeaway cup, the warmth grounding her. Maybe that's why she asked for it in a takeaway cup—so she'd have an escape route if needed. She could still walk away.

But then the door opened. And her heart stuttered. She was here. There was no backing out now.

Lola straightened, forcing herself to rise as the woman approached. She tried for a smile, though her pulse thrummed beneath her skin.

The woman before her was breathtaking, effortlessly so. She had a radiant warmth, her skin catching the soft café light. Her features were delicate yet striking—dark, wide eyes framed by thick lashes, an oval face tapering to a graceful chin. Her hair, dark and wavy, was loosely pinned into a bun at the nape of her neck, with stray strands brushing against her collarbone. A pair of sunglasses perched atop her head, and she wore a denim jacket over a mini sundress, her movements light but confident.

A presence both familiar and strange.

She stopped at the table, her lips parting into a grin. "Lola?"

Lola half-nodded, still bracing herself for what was about to unfold.

"I am *so* sorry," the woman rushed out, exhaling as she brushed a strand of hair back.

"I hope you haven't been waiting too long. *Far out*, the traffic today is out of this world."

She barely paused for breath before continuing, "Mental note to self—" she tapped her temple— "limit movements on Fridays. Seriously, you'd think it was an *exodus* or something." She rolled her eyes dramatically. "And they say Melbourne is one of the most livable cities in the world. *Ha!* Don't get me wrong, I love my Melbs, but *crikey*! What is up with the traffic these days?"

Lola opened her mouth to respond, but before she could, the woman let out a breathy laugh. "Anyway! I'm absolutely *parched*. I'll just grab a drink before we get into it."

She hesitated, then added, "Oh! My bad. I totally forgot to introduce myself." She flashed a sheepish grin, pressing a hand lightly to her chest. "I'm Sheena. And, uh—you haven't been waiting long, right?"

Lola's fingers tightened around her cup. The nerves hadn't entirely settled, but something about Sheena's presence made it easier to breathe, as though they weren't meeting for the first time.

She shook her head. "No, you're fine. I got here with plenty of time to spare. I live just around the corner, so I walked. I hate traffic too, so I know the feeling."

Sheena let out a relieved sigh. "Thank God. And ooh—iced coffee sounds amazing right now. Good call." She winked before making her way to the counter.

Lola sighed slowly. This was *fine*. It was just a meeting.

But as she watched Sheena chat animatedly with the barista, something about the scene felt surreal—like a moment suspended between reality and something else.

A familiarity that made no sense.

Sheena returned moments later, taking a satisfied sip from her drink. "Wow. You weren't kidding—this iced coffee *is* amazing."

Lola smiled, but the weight in her stomach hadn't lifted.

Sheena waved a hand. "Oh, and don't stress about the location. It actually works great. I don't live far from here either. I *thought* I'd be coming from home, but I had a last-minute gig on the other side of town." She shrugged. "I don't mind the extra running around. Perks of getting paid to do it, right?"

She clapped her hands together, leaning slightly forward. "So! What can I help you with? I'm guessing it's something to do with photography for an engagement party?"

Lola's stomach twisted. Right. This was it.

"Er, yeah—I guess," she started hesitantly. But Sheena squinted slightly, tilting her head.

"Wait," she murmured, eyes flicking over Lola's face. "Now that I think about it..." A slow frown formed as though a thought had just taken root. "I swear—you recognized me before I even came over."

Lola's throat tightened.

"Have we met before?" Sheena mused.

Lola gulped. This was it. The moment of truth.

She took a steadying breath, forcing herself to meet Sheena's gaze.

"Sheena, I'm really sorry," she said, voice quieter now.

"But I haven't been completely honest with you."

Chapter Six: The Face-off

The silence between the two women was thick, stretched tight like an invisible wire about to snap. The usual hum of the café faded into a distant murmur as if the world had momentarily stilled, waiting for whatever came next.

Then Sheena spoke, cutting through the tension like a blade.

"What?" Her voice was sharp, incredulous. "I don't understand. What do you mean exactly? Honest about what?"

She scanned the café, her gaze darting around as if she had walked into the middle of an elaborate prank. Any second now, someone would jump out with a camera, laughing, *Gotcha!* But nothing happened. There were no amused onlookers or conspiratorial glances—just the usual mix of patrons, utterly unaware of the unravelling conversation at her table.

She redirected her attention to the woman sitting across from her—Lola.

If that was even her *real* name.

Lola looked composed—too composed. Her white halter-neck top contrasted beautifully against her dark skin, and her long braids framed her face with effortless elegance.

She had a quiet confidence—not showy or arrogant—but it felt like something else was beneath the surface. Something rehearsed as if she had repeatedly played out this moment in her mind, bracing for impact.

A strange flicker of familiarity stirred in Sheena's mind.

Had they met before?

The thought was unsettling.

Sheena had dealt with her fair share of bizarre encounters—prank calls, creepy messages, the occasional weirdo trying to track her down for cake orders that never existed. But this? This was different. This was *real*. Right?

And the worst part? She had walked right into it.

Sheena's stomach tightened. She really needed to be more careful about who she agreed to meet.

Lola hesitated before speaking again, her fingers tightening around her cup. "Okay... well, it's true that I *am* engaged." She swallowed, as if the motion might loosen the words stuck in her throat. "But that's not the real reason you're here."

Sheena stilled, her expression unreadable.

"I'm engaged to someone you were once... involved with." Lola's voice wavered slightly. "I mean, in a relationship with."

The words landed between them like lead, heavy and final.

Sheena didn't move. Didn't blink. The only sign she had heard was the faint tightening of her jaw.

Lola inhaled sharply, the weight of her confession pressing down on her. For a moment, she wished she hadn't said anything at all. *Please don't throw your iced coffee on me,* she thought wildly.

Instead, Sheena leaned back in her chair, her lips curling into a slow, unreadable smile. She lifted her cup, taking a deliberate sip, her gaze never leaving Lola's.

"You're going to need to be a *lot* more specific than that," she said finally, her voice smooth but laced with something sharper. "I've been in 'relationships' with quite a few guys." She raised her hands in exaggerated air quotes, her fingers flicking dismissively in the air.

Lola swallowed, feeling suddenly uncomfortable.

Sheena tilted her head slightly as if weighing her next move. Should she drag this woman through the mud for wasting her time? Should she turn on the venom and make her squirm?

The thought was tempting.

But instead, she crossed her arms, waiting.

Lola hesitated before speaking. "Brett."

Something flickered in Sheena's expression, almost imperceptible.

"Brett Martin?" Lola pressed, her voice quieter now. "I think... you were actually engaged to him at one point."

For a split second, Sheena didn't react. Then, she turned her gaze toward the window, her expression carefully neutral. "Oh. Brett." She said the name as if it were nothing more than an afterthought. "Right."

A beat of silence passed before she spoke again. "That was a while ago. We have nothing to do with each other now." She shrugged. "Things didn't work out. End of."

Lola hesitated, biting her lip. "Can I ask why?"

Sheena's eyes flicked back to her sharply, the warmth draining from her expression.

"Why didn't you ask *him* that?" she countered. "You're the one in a relationship with him."

Lola's pulse quickened.

"Why track me down under some false pretense?" Sheena continued, her voice calm and measured. "Why not just ask your *fiancé* why he and I ended things? Unless, of course..." She leaned forward slightly, her tone shifting into something knowing. "You don't trust the answer he gave you."

Lola felt her stomach twist.

"I completely agree," she admitted, her voice barely above a whisper. "If I were you, I'd probably feel exactly the same."

Sheena huffed out a dry laugh. "Exactly!"

She pushed back from the table. "I'm sorry, but I don't make it a habit of discussing exes—especially not with their current partners." She stood, grabbing her bag.

Panic shot through Lola.

Without thinking, she rose from her seat, hands lifting in a silent plea. "Please, Sheena. Just a few more minutes?" Her voice was raw, unexpectedly desperate.

Sheena hesitated.

For the first time, there was a shift in her guarded expression. Something almost imperceptible.

Slowly, she sat back down. "Five minutes."

With a hint of relief, Lola said, "Thank you."

She hesitated before continuing, her voice quieter now. "I don't have many friends here. I don't know who to talk to about this."

Sheena snorted, shaking her head. Lola ignored the reaction and pushed on.

"Brett and I... I thought we hit it off, but looking back, maybe I was just filling a gap. It *felt* real, but maybe it was just... trauma bonding or whatever they call it." She exhaled shakily. "I was lonely. Still grieving my mum—it's been just over a year."

Sheena's expression flickered, though she masked it quickly. "I'm sorry to hear that," she murmured.

Lola nodded, swallowing hard. "Anyway. I think Brett and I bonded over similar things. He lost a parent, too. Well, sort of."

Sheena's brow furrowed. "Wait, what? He lost his mum?"

Lola hesitated. "Not his mum. His dad." She explained. "He's not dead, but... he's been sick for a long time."

Sheena's posture stiffened.

Then, out of nowhere, she let out a quiet, humourless laugh.

Lola blinked. "What?"

"Oh, how the mighty fall," Sheena murmured, shaking her head, a cold amusement flickering in her dark eyes. "I'm sure he had it coming."

Lola stared at her, thrown by the sudden shift.

The moment lingered between them, charged with something unspoken.

Something fractured.

And for the first time, Lola couldn't shake the feeling that this conversation—this whole encounter—was slipping into something far more complicated than she had anticipated.

Chapter Seven: Things Go South

For a few seconds, Lola was sure that Sheena hadn't heard her correctly. Or that she hadn't meant to respond in that way.

She blinked, staring at her.

"Er... his father is *really* sick," she repeated, as if clarifying would somehow change the moment.

"And thank goodness for that," Sheena said. Her voice was cool, void of remorse. "Maybe there *is* some sort of justice in the world after all."

Lola's spine stiffened. "Wow. Did you hate him that much?"

Sheena studied her for a long moment, her eyes unreadable. Then, tilting her head slightly, she asked, "Did you ever meet his dad before he fell ill?"

"No." Lola shook her head. "The accident—it happened before I met Brett. But I did see him once... at the hospital."

She hesitated, her voice faltering as the memory surfaced.

She hadn't let herself dwell on that visit, but now, it rose inside her like a ghost.

The hospital had been suffocating in its monotony—a place caught in limbo between life and death. The intensive care unit felt like a void, where time stretched and folded in on itself, where hope was measured in beeping monitors and the slow, rhythmic hiss of ventilators.

She remembered Brett's father lying motionless in the bed, his body swallowed by the crisp white sheets. His complexion had been a sickly, pallid grey, a stark contrast to the man she had imagined—someone larger than life, formidable. Seeing him like that had unsettled her.

And it had stirred something else, something darker.

A strange relief.

Her own mother had died suddenly—a brain aneurysm, the doctors had said. There had been no bedside vigils, no weeks or months of slow decline. Just here one moment, gone the next. She had been spared the kind of suffering that Brett and his mother were now enduring.

Sheena's voice cut through her thoughts, pulling her back.

"The man was so bloody controlling."

Lola blinked, refocusing.

"I got the sense he was... strict," she said carefully, choosing her words. "Brett doesn't talk much about him, but from what little I know, I formed a picture of someone quite... formidable."

Sheena scoffed, shaking her head. "*Strict* would've been a kindness. No, he was manipulative. Controlling. He made everyone's life miserable."

Lola leaned forward slightly; her curiosity piqued. "Why do you say that?"

Sheena opened her mouth as if to speak, then hesitated. Her expression shuttered, as though she had said too much.

"I think I've said enough," she muttered. Then, with a slight, knowing smirk, she added, "But maybe now that he's out of the way, you and Brett can have some peace."

Lola frowned. "I never met his dad before the accident, so that's not the issue. His mum, though..." She trailed off, her brow furrowing. "She's a bit... odd. Not terrible or meddling, really. But the few times we've met, she's been distant. Like she's trapped in a cycle of sadness and loss, always carrying it with her."

Shaking her head, trying to gather her thoughts, she said, "And honestly? I get the feeling she doesn't *like* me much. Not in an obvious way, but... it's like I make her uncomfortable somehow."

Sheena leaned back in her chair, crossing her arms. "Well, you can never be a hundred per cent sure about people. There's always *some* risk when you commit to someone. That's the gamble, right?"

Her tone was firm, but her expression softened slightly.

Then—

A loud crash shattered the moment.

Lola jumped as the sharp clatter of breaking ceramic rang through the café. A tray of mugs had hit the floor behind the counter, shards scattering in all directions.

A barista groaned in frustration as another scrambled to clean up the mess.

Lola's heart was still pounding, but it wasn't the noise itself that unsettled her.

It was Sheena.

Her face had gone ghostly pale, her pupils blown wide. Her fingers clenched against the table, knuckles whitening.

"Sheena?" Lola's voice was cautious now. "Are you okay?"

Sheena didn't respond.

She was staring at something that wasn't there—something distant, something only she could see.

Then, suddenly, she pushed back her chair, the legs scraping loudly against the floor. Her movements were sharp, almost panicked.

"I... I need to go," she stammered, her voice barely above a whisper.

Lola reached out instinctively. "Wait—Sheena, what's wrong?"

Sheena shook her head, her expression unreadable, her breathing slightly uneven.

"Just... forget it," she muttered.

She turned, stepping away.

And without thinking, the words left Lola's lips.

"I think I might be pregnant."

Sheena's steps faltered mid-stride.

She stopped. Slowly, she turned back, her expression shifting—part bewilderment, part intrigue.

Lola took a deep breath, unsure whether she had just made a mistake.

"I haven't tested yet, but if the missed period is a clue..."

Lola said slowly. "I thought I was being careful, but..." She trailed off, shaking her head.

Sheena's gaze flickered with something—curiosity, maybe even concern. "And that's why you want to know more about Brett and what happened in the past?"

Lola nodded.

"Does he know?" Sheena asked.

Lola shook her head. "I want to be sure I'm *actually* pregnant first. But also, I want to fill in some gaps where Brett is concerned."

Sheena's expression darkened. "Gaps?"

Lola sighed and responded, "It's like a part of Brett is locked away somewhere, and I'm only seeing this carefully curated version of him, not the real him. Warts and all."

She glanced at Sheena, searching her face for any flicker of understanding, some unspoken acknowledgment that she knew precisely what Lola meant.

Sheena nodded slowly, letting out a soft sigh. "Brett was definitely the quiet type. I could talk for hours throughout our relationship, and he'd just sit there, content to listen. I mean, I can be quite the chatterbox, so maybe that worked well for me," she said with a faint smile.

She shifted in her seat, shrugging lightly.

"I don't know. I guess I was too distracted dealing with his dictator dad to notice anything else. But yeah, Brett could be a bit... timid. I told him as much. I thought it held him back sometimes, you know? But even then, I always felt like something else was going on—like he was carrying this weight. He never said it outright, but I could tell he was nursing heartbreak from his previous relationship."

Sheena hesitated, glancing at Lola as if seeking permission to continue.

"You know, with the mother of his child—Chrissie?" Her voice softened, tentative.

Lola nodded, her expression thoughtful. Chrissie was Brett's teenage daughter from his first serious relationship, which had ended abruptly. All Lola knew was that Chrissie's mum wasn't in the picture.

Brett had hinted at it once, saying she wasn't ready to be a mother, having had Chrissie when she was pretty young. He had been evasive about the details, and Lola had quickly realized it was a sensitive subject. Still, a small part of her felt hurt that Brett hadn't trusted her enough to confide in her about something so important.

Chrissie had always been a free spirit—so unlike her reserved father. She was endlessly talkative, full of curiosity, and always ready for a chat. Lola had grown fond of her over time despite the complicated and delicate balance of her role in the girl's life.

Sheena's lips curved slightly, her gaze turning inward, softening with nostalgia.

"She was so young back then. She used to love playing hide-and-seek. She wanted to play it every single day. And she was good at it, too! Sometimes, she'd hide so well that I'd forget I was supposed to be looking for her." She let out a small chuckle, shaking her head at the memory.

Lola smiled, warmth flickering across her face.

"Yeah... that sounds like her."

A quiet settled between them, the kind that wasn't uncomfortable but held the weight of something unspoken.

The background murmur of the café, the distant clatter of dishes, and the low hum of music drifted around them like white noise, yet neither woman seemed fully present in the space. They were somewhere else—somewhere in the past.

Then Lola spoke, her voice quieter, more thoughtful.

"She's outgrown that now. She's a teenager, so she mostly hides away in her room these days. I don't see her that often. But when we do spend time together... it's nice."

Sheena tilted her head slightly as if considering that, then exhaled a slow, measured breath.

"I have to admit, I struggled with being an... auxiliary mum," she said, her fingers absently playing with the straw in her drink jar. The words felt strange, even now.

"I guess that was part of the reason why Brett and I didn't work out. I couldn't see it being my life forever. I wanted to do more, to be more. And honestly..." She hesitated, her gaze dropping to the table, watching the condensation slide down the side of her glass.

"I don't think motherhood is my thing. I mean, not in that way. I felt like Brett and Chrissie deserved someone who could give them everything, and I just... wasn't that woman."

She twisted the straw between her fingers, the ice shifting against the glass with a soft clink.

Lola didn't answer right away.

Outside, a breeze stirred the leaves of the trees lining the sidewalk, sending them dancing against the window. Sunlight flickered through the shifting branches, casting moving shadows across the table.

"I get it," Lola finally said, her voice steady but her expression unreadable.

For a moment, neither of them spoke. The past and present blurred together, slipping between their words, their silences. The air between them carried the weight of something unsaid—something just out of reach.

Sheena shook her head slowly, a flicker of regret crossing her face.

"I wasn't ready for that life. I didn't want to hold them back, and I didn't want to lose myself trying to fit into a life I wasn't sure I could handle."

Her voice softened as she trailed off, her words settling between them like the quiet ripples of a stone dropped in still water.

"I guess it's not something to be taken casually," Lola said, a flash of anxiety washing over her as she thought about the unused test kit in her bathroom drawer. She had debated using it this morning, but the fear had stopped her.

"Do you have any kids?" Sheena asked, as if somehow reading Lola's mind.

Now, it was Lola's turn to feel the weight of the conversation shift. She suddenly became aware that she was sitting across from a woman she had no real idea about—besides her being Brett's ex.

It took Lola a while before replying succinctly. "No. Why?" she asked, somewhat defensively.

"Just asking," Sheena said, her expression unreadable but tinged with something curious.

She continued after a pause.

"But... you don't mind spending time with her? With Chrissie, I mean?"

Lola hesitated, her gaze drifting as she reflected on the question.

"No, why should it be a problem? It's fine," she said finally.

"It's nice having her around sometimes. I can't say I mind." Her voice softened, and she smiled faintly. "I've always envied women with daughters, you know? There's that bond some mothers have with their girls, especially when they're at a certain age. You can have proper conversations with them and share things in a way that's... different. It's something I've always imagined must be special."

She paused, glancing at Sheena before adding, "But it sounds like it wasn't quite like that for you."

Sheena scrunched her nose slightly as though weighing her thoughts. "Hmm... not really, no," she said slowly.

Lola nodded, her tone understanding.

"I can imagine that being difficult." She hesitated for a moment before asking, "But did he ever talk much about her? His ex, I mean?"

Sheena shook her head. "Not really. To be honest, I didn't ask much about his past. What's the point in dwelling on things you can't control?" She shrugged lightly.

"The little I learned about her came out when Brett was stressed or frustrated; even then, it was vague. But from what I gathered, she's very much out of the picture. I think she might've returned to the UK—where she's originally from."

"I see," Lola said quietly.

Sheena shrugged again and said, "Maybe the distance helped her separate herself, you know? Like I said, some women just aren't maternal. They're not cut out for that life."

"Then maybe she shouldn't have had a child in the first place," Lola said, the words slipping out before she could stop herself.

She winced internally, realizing how judgmental she sounded.

Sheena's face tightened instantly, her irritation apparent.

"Judgey much?" she said, her tone sharp. "Ugh, I can't stand it when people just pass judgment on things they know nothing about."

"I'm sorry," Lola said quickly, lightly closing her eyes and rubbing her temples. "I really shouldn't have said that."

"No, you shouldn't have," Sheena replied coolly, crossing her arms. She gave Lola a pointed look, her voice hardening.

Lola hesitated. "It's just that he has a daughter whose mother is completely out of the picture. It's like she doesn't exist. I want to be sure she left *of her own volition*. Not because she was afraid. Or threatened."

Something flashed across Sheena's face. A shadow of something unspoken.

Lola pressed on. "I've read nightmare stories about women feeling trapped. Having children with men, only to realize too late that they were in too deep." Her voice wavered slightly. "I don't want that."

Sheena studied her carefully. "You're not an Australian citizen?"

Lola shook her head. "No. Not yet. I'm a permanent resident, but my doctorate has kept me from finalizing my citizenship."

Sheena let out a soft chuckle—though it had no humour. "So quick to judge Chrissie's mum for leaving, yet you're afraid of the same thing."

Lola's stomach twisted. "I didn't mean—"

"You *assumed* she was selfish. That she walked away without a care." Sheena's gaze was cool, detached. "But maybe she wasn't as selfish as you think. Maybe there were circumstances beyond her control that drove her away."

Lola was about to press further when a sudden noise interrupted her - A chair scraping loudly against the floor. A fork clattering onto a plate. A burst of laughter from a table nearby.

Sheena flinched, her shoulders tensing as though the noise had cut through her skin.

Her gaze darted toward the café entrance. Then, without another word, she turned on her heel and was gone.

Lola sat frozen, her pulse still racing.

What the *hell* had just happened?

Chapter Eight: A Night of Reflection

Lola jolted awake, her chest heaving, the damp fabric of her nightie clinging to her skin. The air in her room felt stifling, the lingering shadows of the dream clawing at the edges of her consciousness.

It was *that* dream again—the one that returned like an uninvited guest, familiar yet no less terrifying.

In the dream, she stood on the balcony of an old, weathered house. The cracked railings and faded wood hinted at its age, yet it felt strangely comforting, as if she belonged there. The house overlooked an endless expanse of ocean.

At first, the view was idyllic: the sun danced on the surface of the shimmering waves, and the soft hum of the sea breeze mingled with the call of distant gulls. The sky stretched vast and blue, unmarred by a single cloud.

She always began by leaning on the balcony, basking in the warmth of the scene, her fingers tracing the splintered edge of the railing. Then it came—a voice calling her name from somewhere inside the house, faint yet insistent.

She turned her head, just for a moment, searching for the source. The voice was never clear, but it tugged at her, pulling her attention away.

But when she looked back toward the ocean, the world had shifted.

The vibrant blue sky had vanished, replaced by a menacing shade of grey that churned like molten ash. The air felt heavier, colder, and electric with foreboding.

The waves on the horizon began to rise, unnaturally high, towering against the skyline like liquid giants. Their roars grew deafening, drowning out the wind, the birds—and *even her heartbeat.*

She wanted to move, to run, but her feet were rooted to the weathered planks of the balcony. Her mouth opened in a scream, but no sound escaped. The waves surged closer, monstrous and unrelenting, their shadow consuming the light.

And then, with a thunderous crash, they swallowed her whole.

Lola sat frozen in bed, her skin prickling as if the icy water from her dream still clung to her. Her breath came shallow, her heart pounding like a distant drum.

She stared into the dimly lit room, her body stiff, until the sharp buzz of her phone shattered the stillness.

Groaning, she rubbed her temples, a dull ache spreading behind her eyes. The screen of her phone glowed faintly, face down on the bedside table. She reached for it with a twinge of apprehension, half-expecting Brett's name to flash across the screen. He'd called so many times these past few days; each missed call added another layer of guilt.

But it wasn't Brett. It was Sheena.

Lola frowned, recognizing the peculiar combination of zeros and ones.

"Hello?" she said hesitantly, her voice still thick with sleep. For a moment, she wondered if this was another dream, the kind where she thought she was awake but wasn't.

"Hey, Lola. What are you up to?" Sheena's voice came through, far too casual for the late hour.

"Sheena? Is that you?" Lola asked, sitting upright. "Do you even know what time it is?"

"Yeah, it's me," Sheena replied breezily. "And, of course, I know the time. It's 11:33 p.m. Don't tell me you were already asleep?"

Lola closed her eyes, the ache in her temples intensifying.

"Sheena, 11:33 at night is a perfectly reasonable time for anyone to be asleep. What's *not* reasonable is calling someone you barely know at this hour."

"Okay, fair point," Sheena admitted, her tone light but slightly breathless. "But you did kind of crash into my life unannounced, so maybe this is just me returning the favour."

Lola sighed, conceding with a slight nod. "Fine. What do you want?"

"I thought we could talk," Sheena said, her voice softening. "Our earlier chat stirred up some things I'd buried. And besides, I think you owe me a drink after that little stunt you pulled."

"A drink?" Lola couldn't help but laugh, the sound dry and incredulous. "You *are* kidding, right?"

"Nope. I'm dead serious. I'm in the mood for a vodka cranberry, and guess what? You're buying."

Lola pinched the bridge of her nose, exhaling sharply.

"Sheena, I'm sorry for barging into your life today, but I'm exhausted. The last thing I feel like doing is getting dressed to meet my partner's *ex* for a drink."

"Please," Sheena said quietly, almost pleading.

The sudden vulnerability in her tone caught Lola off guard. She'd expected sass or sarcasm—not this.

Lola hesitated, her fingers tracing idle patterns on the blanket.

She was awake now, and a part of her—one she didn't fully understand—felt compelled to meet Sheena again. Their earlier conversation had left her with questions, little nagging thoughts that wouldn't quite let go.

She let out a slow breath.

"Fine," she said. "Where are we meeting?"

…———— ✠ ————…

Sheena had chosen a cellar bar on Bourke Street, tucked inconspicuously between a boutique bookstore and a shuttered tailor's shop.

Lola wasn't the type to frequent bars—she couldn't even remember the last time she'd set foot in one. For one, she didn't have many friends to share impulsive nights out with, and Brett was far from a social butterfly.

In truth, Brett wasn't much of a party person at all. She used to be more spontaneous back in college when late-night adventures felt like a natural extension of her youth. But that version of herself seemed like a distant stranger now.

The question of what to wear plagued her for nearly twenty minutes before she settled on a "safe but cool" option: a black satin shirt dress paired with chunky heeled ankle boots.

As she rifled through her wardrobe, she noticed how many black outfits she had accumulated over the years, like a quiet, sartorial surrender to routine.

At the last minute, she grabbed a scarf from the hall stand, the evening air having shifted from the warm embrace of the afternoon to a sharp chill that nipped at her resolve.

The Uber ride had been uneventful until the driver dropped her off across the street from the bar, forcing her to jaywalk in her boots. She huffed quietly in annoyance as she waited for a lull in the sparse traffic, muttering under her breath about his lack of courtesy. Making a U-turn wouldn't have killed him.

Her irritation dissipated as she crossed the dimly lit street, where the faint hum of life emanated from the bar's narrow staircase.

Sheena was waiting at the entrance, her silhouette backlit by the golden streetlamp overhead. A wisp of smoke curled around her as she took a final drag from her vape. There was something entirely unsurprising about this—the image of Sheena vaping felt as natural as if it had been part of her introduction.

"I was starting to think you wouldn't show," Sheena said with a wry smile, her eyes narrowing slightly as she exhaled a plume of vapour that hung momentarily between them.

She flicked the device into her bag with a flourish and motioned toward the narrow staircase. "Come on, let's see what kind of trouble we can find tonight."

"I wasn't sure I'd find the place," Lola admitted, her voice laced with mild defensiveness. "Have you been here before?"

"A few times," Sheena replied, her tone as nonchalant as her appearance—a brown leather corset that clung to her like armour, black ripped jeans frayed just enough to look intentional, and boots that seemed made for stomping through midnight adventures.

As they descended, the brick walls grew cooler to the touch, the faint thrum of bass music vibrating through them like a heartbeat. The narrow and uneven stairs seemed to carry them into a different dimension—a hidden pocket of the city far removed from the world above.

The cellar bar was a small, intimate cocoon of muted light and shadows. Pools of golden light from industrial pendant lamps hung low over the tables, casting halos that illuminated polished wood surfaces and glinting bottles.

The bar itself stretched along one side of the room, its counter a mosaic of scratches and stories, backlit with a warm amber glow that turned every drink into a liquid gem.

The air was alive with quiet energy. Conversations buzzed softly, merging with the velvety strains of a jazz tune that floated from unseen speakers.

Patrons were scattered across the room—some perched on barstools, leaning conspiratorially toward the bartender, while others reclined in mismatched armchairs that looked like they'd been salvaged from a bygone era.

In one corner, a group of friends erupted into laughter, their mirth spilling into the otherwise hushed atmosphere. Across the room, a couple huddled close, their faces half-hidden in shadow, their murmurs too soft to decipher but heavy with meaning.

Lola felt a flicker of nervous excitement. The room carried a quiet rebellion, like it was a sanctuary for misfits and dreamers who craved something more. It wasn't just a bar—it was a refuge, a place where time seemed to stretch, and the boundaries of the everyday world dissolved.

The bartender worked with practised ease, moving like he was conducting a quiet symphony. Glasses clinked as he poured drinks, the sound punctuating the murmur of voices.

Sheena led the way, her strides confident and purposeful as she navigated the maze of scattered chairs and low tables.

She moved with the ease of someone who belonged here, her presence fluid, almost magnetic, as if she was a part of the bar's rhythm.

Lola followed a step behind, her pace slower, her heels clicking faintly against the stone floor. The sound seemed to echo her hesitation, like a quiet drumbeat in the shadows and soft golden light.

As she watched Sheena ahead of her, she felt a strange feeling of déjà vu. Like she had been here before. Something about being in Sheena's company felt familiar, like she had known her for longer than she had, and this was not their first time hanging out together. It felt nice.

They chose a pair of armchairs tucked in a corner, just far enough from the bustle of the bar to feel private. The upholstery was threadbare but inviting, with mismatched cushions piled haphazardly, adding a cozy, lived-in charm to their little refuge.

"I guess I'm taking orders," Sheena announced, settling back into her chair and crossing her legs with practised nonchalance.

"Still in the mood for a vodka cranberry?" Lola asked.

"Yup. Although…" Sheena paused dramatically, flicking her hair away from her face and letting her gaze wander across the room.

"I think I'm starting to crave a mojito. That'll be my second drink of countless drinks for the night." Her lips curled into a mischievous smile as her eyes lingered on a group of men at the bar. "And who knows? Maybe I'll get lucky tonight. Some of these blokes are *quite* fetching."

Lola arched an eyebrow, her tone dry. "Seriously? Is that why you dragged me out here tonight? To be your wingwoman?"

Sheena let out a rich laugh, waving her off with a dismissive hand. "Oh, come on. I'm kidding – well, *kind of.* But hey, maybe I'll recommend something a little stronger for you, too. Or maybe…" Sheena's gaze flickered downward, lingering meaningfully on Lola's midriff. '…maybe you should stick to a mocktail. You know, *just in case.*"

Lola groaned inwardly, shooting Sheena a sharp look before heading to the bar. She returned a few minutes later, balancing a vodka cranberry for Sheena and a virgin piña colada for herself. Sheena accepted her drink with a knowing smirk.

"Well," she said, her tone teasing as her eyes rested on Lola's untouched glass. "I take it you haven't done the test yet."

Lola shook her head, looking away. "Not yet, no."

Sheena rolled her eyes, leaning forward to sip her drink. "Honestly, I don't get it. Just put yourself out of your misery and do the damn test. Why drag it out?"

Lola hesitated, the words hovering on the tip of her tongue. She wanted to snap back at her, to remind Sheena it was none of her business, but she bit back a retort. After all, she'd been the one to share this little secret in the first place.

"I just… I want to pretend for a little longer that it might not be real. That it might not be possible," she admitted softly.

"Well," Sheena said with a shrug, her tone laced with sarcasm. "If you're pretending, you might as well do it properly. Get yourself a *real* drink!"

Lola sighed, the exhaustion creeping into her voice. "Why *did* you call me out, Sheena?"

Sheena leaned back in her chair, exhaling slowly. "Besides needing a distraction from a crappy day? I guess I'm curious about you. About you and Brett. He wasn't a bad boyfriend, but we were never really a good match.

Breaking up was harder on him than it was on me, but I think it was for the best. I couldn't have made him happy."

Sheena shook her head, tucking a strand of hair behind her ear. "Seeing you today, though... I get it. You fit. I see why he'd be with you. He's a good guy, and I don't think you should call off the engagement. Unless there's another reason?"

Lola studied Sheena for a moment, unsure how to respond. "Why do you think we fit?"

Sheena tilted her head thoughtfully. "I don't know. Maybe it's just the vibe I'm getting from you. You seem reserved and mellow. Not like me—I'm all over the place." She let out a self-deprecating laugh.

Lola gave a faint smile though her thoughts churned. She knew what Sheena meant. The irony was that she often wished she was more like Sheena—spontaneous, daring, talkative, and confident.

"Sometimes I think Brett and I are too alike," she said, tracing her finger along the condensation on her glass. "Opposites attract, right?" She hesitated before adding, almost shyly, "Besides... I can see why he was drawn to you. You're gorgeous."

Sheena laughed, a warm, throaty sound. "Oh, come on! You're a babe yourself." She winked at Lola.

Lola smiled, though there was a hint of sadness in her eyes. "Sometimes, I feel invisible. Brett was the first guy to really... see me and genuinely care."

"Was he your first boyfriend?" Sheena asked, her voice softer now.

Lola nodded, a faint blush creeping up her cheeks. The weight of the past settled over her like a fog. "What about you?" she asked quickly, changing the subject. "Are you seeing anyone?"

Sheena hesitated, her fingers toying with the rim of her glass. "Kind of. I like to keep my options open," she said lightly, though her eyes betrayed a flicker of something deeper.

The story spilled out before she could stop herself—the kiss with Alex, the unexpected intensity, and the confusion it left in its wake.

Lola listened intently, her expression thoughtful. "Sounds like you had a connection," she said. "But maybe it's better to let it go. He doesn't sound like he was ever truly yours. Do you think you loved him?"

Sheena sighed, her confidence faltering for just a moment. "I don't know. He came into my life when I wasn't looking for anyone, but... he made me feel something. By the time I thought we could make it work, he'd moved on." She paused, swirling the last of her drink in the glass. "Maybe it's time to close that chapter. Do something else with my life."

Before the silence could stretch too far, Sheena straightened up, a determined grin spreading across her face. "Alright, enough of this self-pity! It's *more rounds o'clock* -My treat! And I'm *not* getting you another bloody piña colada!"

Lola laughed, the tension easing as Sheena strode toward the bar, her confidence blazing like a beacon.

As Sheena headed toward the bar, Lola watched her go, momentarily lost in thought. Sheena moved with an effortless grace, her confidence almost tangible, lighting up the dim space like a spark. It was hard not to admire her boldness—her ability to seize moments without overthinking.

Lola sighed and leaned back in her chair; her drink clutched loosely in her hands. Brett's face floated into her mind, steady and familiar. Theirs had been a quiet, steady kind of love. One that didn't flare brightly but burned with a dependable glow.

Sheena had called it a good fit, but sometimes Lola wondered if that was enough. Did a "good fit' mean a happy future?

She knew Brett loved her—had always made her feel seen in ways no one else had before. That was rare, wasn't it? Precious, even. And yet, sitting here, surrounded by the hum of the bar and the infectious energy Sheena radiated, Lola couldn't help but feel a pang of doubt.

She traced the rim of her glass absentmindedly. There had been a time when she longed for spontaneity, for a rush of passion that made her feel alive in ways Brett never quite did. Brett was reliable, thoughtful, and kind. But was he *exciting?* Or was she simply the kind of person who didn't need excitement? Sheena's words lingered in her mind: *You seem reserved, mellow. Not like me—I'm all over the place.*

Maybe Sheena was right. Maybe Brett and Sheena were too mismatched to work, and maybe that's why Lola and Brett made sense. But it didn't stop her from wondering what life might look like if she let herself be a little more like

Sheena—fearless, unreserved, and unafraid to follow the currents of her heart, wherever they might lead.

Across the room, Sheena leaned against the bar, laughing at something the bartender said. Lola smiled faintly. It was impossible to ignore Sheena's magnetism, the way she drew people in. It was no wonder Brett had fallen for her once.

When Sheena returned with their drinks, her face carried a flicker of something more subdued, like a shadow she hadn't been able to shake. She handed Lola her drink and settled back into her chair with a sigh.

"You okay?" Lola asked, the concern in her voice genuine.

Sheena hesitated, swirling her drink as though searching its depths for an answer. The dim light of the bar cast shifting shadows across her face, her expression unreadable yet layered with something fragile.

"Do you ever feel like... you're stuck between who you were and who you're supposed to be?" she asked, her voice soft but weighted.

Lola's brow furrowed slightly. She hadn't expected the evening to take such a reflective turn. "What do you mean?" she asked, tilting her head as though angling for a clearer view of Sheena's thoughts.

Sheena's lips curved into a wistful smile, tinged with a sadness she didn't bother to mask. "Alex made me feel like I could be something more," she began, her voice trembling slightly.

"Like I could let go of the chaos and just... be happy in the moment." A quiet breath escaped her. "But I didn't realize it until it was too late."

Her voice grew softer. "By the time I thought I was ready, he'd moved on." She hesitated, the weight of regret heavy in her tone. "And now, I'm stuck wondering if I missed my chance at something real."

Lola's heart ached for her, though she couldn't quite tell if it was sympathy or envy. Sheena's life seemed so vibrant, so full of possibility, even in its messiness.

There was an allure to Sheena's chaos, a rawness that Lola found both intimidating and captivating.

Lola couldn't help but wonder if Sheena envied her in return—the stability of her relationship with Brett, the security of knowing where her life was headed.

"Do you regret it?" Lola asked quietly, the question feeling heavy in the air between them.

Sheena considered it for a moment, her gaze distant. "Regret? No. Not exactly," she said finally. "Alex came into my life for a reason, even if it was just to show me what I'm capable of feeling. But I think... I think it's time to stop looking back. I'm tired of being stuck in a loop."

Lola nodded, though her thoughts were more tangled. Did she feel stuck too? Or was she just overthinking, as usual?

She lifted her glass to her lips, letting the sweetness of the drink wash over her tongue and distract her, if only for a moment.

Sheena's eyes sharpened, catching Lola's hesitation. A small, knowing smile played on her lips. "You're thinking too much. Stop overanalyzing and just live a little, okay? That's my motto for tonight."

Lola laughed softly, the sound more an exhale than a genuine expression of amusement. "Easier said than done."

Sheena clinked her glass against Lola's with a mischievous grin. "Then stick with me, and I'll show you how it's done."

Chapter Nine: Dance with Me

As the night progressed, Lola couldn't shake the sense that the conversation had left something unspoken between them. A shared vulnerability, perhaps, or just the quiet understanding that neither of them had it all figured out.

Sheena might project confidence, and Lola might cling to stability, but beneath it all, they were two women trying to make sense of their lives.

And in this dimly lit bar, tucked away from the rest of the world, it felt like enough for Lola. But it seemed Sheena had other plans.

Sheena drained the rest of her drink in one swift motion, her eyes lighting up with sudden energy. "Come on," she said, standing abruptly. "I have somewhere else we can go. It's much more upbeat than here. Since we're already out of our beds and homes, we might as well make good use of it. The night is still young."

Lola glanced at her watch, suppressing a groan. "Young? Hardly. It's well past its prime. It's after midnight, Sheena. My bed is calling me. I can almost hear it whispering my name."

Sheena's laugh was low and teasing. "Stop being such a grandma. Even old ladies have fun. Come on." She grabbed her bag and walked away with a slight wobble, leaving Lola with no choice but to follow.

"Where are we going?" Lola asked, her voice laced with dubiousness.

"Where else? A nightclub," Sheena replied, her grin wicked. "Time to see what moves you've got. Or are you worried your sweet fiancé wouldn't approve?"

Lola rolled her eyes but couldn't suppress a smile. "I'm not worried about Brett. I'm worried about my feet. They're not as young as they used to be."

Sheena chuckled. "Don't worry, Nana. This place has the kind of music that makes you forget all about your aching feet."

The two women walked through the city's narrow streets: the air alive with the hum of late-night revellers. They passed small alleyways where groups of friends laughed too loudly, stumbled slightly, and leaned on each other for support.

Bars and cafés still welcomed patrons, their lights spilling out onto the pavement like invitations. The city felt electric, charged with the kind of energy that only existed in the early hours of the morning.

"What is it with you and basement bars and clubs?" Lola asked, her tone half-teasing. "Did you live as a subterranean in a past life?"

Sheena smirked. "Maybe. There's just something about them. They're a little hidden, a little clandestine. It makes everything feel more exciting, you know?"

Lola's reply was drowned out as they approached their destination. The thumping bass of techno music reached them even before they saw the club's entrance, tucked discreetly beneath an unassuming building on Flinders Lane.

A small, nondescript sign marked the spot, its letters glowing faintly in neon blue. Sheena shot Lola a triumphant look as if to say, *"I told you this was a great idea."*

As they descended the narrow staircase, the music grew louder, each beat vibrating through the walls and into Lola's chest. The anticipation was almost tangible, a hum that buzzed in the air between them. Lola couldn't help but feel a flicker of excitement despite her reservations. This wasn't her usual scene, but maybe... just maybe... Sheena was right. Maybe it was time to stop overthinking and start living.

The club was dark and packed, bodies swaying in rhythm to the hypnotic pulse of the music. Neon lights flashed across the room, painting everything in shades of electric blue and pink.

Sheena's energy seemed to double the moment they stepped inside. She grabbed Lola's hand and pulled her through the crowd, weaving expertly past clusters of dancers who had started going wild as the DJ played *Soweto*, an Afro-fusion song that had gone viral earlier that year.

Sheena's flirtatious nature surfaced almost immediately. She caught the eye of a tall man leaning against the bar, his dark shirt clinging to his frame in the heat of the room. She sent him a sultry smile, tilting her head just enough to let her hair fall over one shoulder. Within moments, he was beside her, the two of them exchanging easy banter that Lola couldn't hear over the pounding music.

Lola lingered on the edge of the dance floor, watching Sheena with a mix of amusement and disbelief. Sheena moved with an effortless confidence, her laughter rising above the music as the man leaned in closer.

Lola, by contrast, felt out of place. The bass reverberated through her, but she couldn't quite bring herself to lose control, to let the music take over the way everyone else seemed to.

Lola headed to the bar to get a glass of Diet Coke. She sipped it slowly, letting the sharp bubbles distract her from the awkwardness she felt. Sheena caught her eye from across the room and gave her an exaggerated wink, her expression saying, "See? Easy."

Lola couldn't help but laugh, shaking her head. Sheena was in her element, and while Lola felt more like a spectator than a participant, there was something freeing about being here—about stepping out of her comfort zone, even if just a little.

Eventually, Sheena made her way back to Lola, her cheeks flushed and her grin impossibly wide. "See? Told you it'd be fun," she said, slightly breathless.

"For you, maybe," Lola teased. "You're practically running the place. Me? I'm just trying not to get trampled."

Sheena laughed, slinging an arm around Lola's shoulders. "You're overthinking again. Just let go. One dance. Come on, I'll even be your partner."

Lola hesitated, but the infectious energy in Sheena's eyes was hard to resist. With a sigh and a small smile, she allowed herself to be dragged onto the dance floor, the music swelling around them like a tide.

For the first few moments, Lola moved awkwardly, unsure what to do with her hands, feet, and body. But then, she glanced at Sheena, who was twirling, laughing, and unapologetically alive. Something in Lola shifted. She let the music take her, let the beat guide her movements. She wasn't as fluid as Sheena, but it didn't matter. She felt lighter, freer, as though the music was unravelling something inside her.

When the song ended, the two women were breathless, their cheeks flushed and their smiles wide. Sheena threw an arm around Lola and leaned in close so she could be heard over the next track. "You did it. You actually danced."

Lola laughed, her heart racing from more than just the exertion. "I guess I did."

As they left the club hours later, the city quiet and bathed in the soft glow of streetlights, Lola felt a strange sense of contentment. Sheena squeezed her arm as they walked side by side. "See? A night like this can remind you how alive you are."

Lola nodded, her smile small but genuine. For the first time in a long time, she felt like she wasn't just existing. She was living. And that, she realized, was more than enough for now.

Chapter Ten: Brett

Brett sat on the edge of his bed, his phone clutched in his hand, scrolling through the unanswered messages. Each blue tick-less bubble seemed to taunt him, a cruel reminder of her growing distance.

His voice messages, once a source of comfort between them, now hung in limbo, unacknowledged. He sighed deeply, his chest tightening with the kind of ache that comes when you realize you might already be too late.

Is this it? He wondered. *The end?*

It was a feeling he knew too well—this sense of losing something before he truly had it. *Déjà vu* wrapped itself around him like an unwelcome shadow. It was a cruel twist—every time he thought he was finally finding his footing in a relationship, something would slip, the ground vanishing beneath him.

His thoughts wandered back to their last real conversation.

They had been in his apartment, a rare quiet evening when the outside world had felt a little further away. He had been at his desk in the study, fine-tuning a project for work, when she had appeared in the doorway, silhouetted by the golden light of the hall. She crossed the room with an effortless grace that always caught him off guard, settling herself on his lap without a word.

She had wrapped her arms around his neck, and they stayed that way for a long moment—his hands resting on her waist, her cheek against his. He remembered the faint scent of lavender in her hair and the warmth of her body against him.

It had felt like the distance between them had vanished for a brief time.

Then she had shifted, her gaze sweeping over the room until it landed on the portrait hanging on the wall—a striking piece, its bold colours softened by delicate brushstrokes.

"I love that portrait," she said, her voice tinged with curiosity. She stood, walking over to the painting. Tilting her head, she squinted to make out the signature scrawled in an elegant flourish at the bottom corner.

"Does that say... Hannah?" she asked, glancing back at him.

Brett felt his stomach clench, a reflexive pang of discomfort. He nodded. "Yeah."

Her brow furrowed slightly, and then a flicker of realization crossed her face. "Wait... was she your ex? You did say she was an artist."

He hesitated, the air between them growing heavier. Finally, he forced the words out. "Yeah. She was."

Lola took a step back, her gaze moving from him to the portrait and back again.

"Wow," she said softly, her tone unreadable. "You must still really like her if you've kept one of her paintings on your wall."

Brett opened his mouth to respond, but nothing came.

What could he say? That the painting was more than just a piece of art? That it was a fragment of a past he didn't know how to let go of, even if he didn't want to return to it?

The silence between them had stretched thick with unspoken truths and misunderstandings.

...— — ⚜ — —...

Brett's thoughts drifted to the last time he had visited his mum. The memory was sharp and vivid and weighed heavily on him.

They had just returned from the hospital after visiting his dad, whose condition seemed to cast an oppressive shadow over everything.

Dinner that evening had been subdued, the atmosphere heavy and mournful, as if the hospital's sorrow had followed them home.

For a while, they had eaten in silence, the clinking of cutlery against plates the only sound in the room. Then his mum broke the silence, her voice gentle but firm.

She looked at him intently, her gaze piercing. "How long do you intend to keep this up? With her?"

Brett's stomach tightened. He glanced at her briefly, then returned his focus to the half-eaten meal before him. She had made his favourite dish—tuna mornay. Usually, he would have polished it off in minutes, but tonight, he had no appetite. He had been pushing the food around his plate, his mind too preoccupied to enjoy it.

"It's obvious it's weighing on your mind, Brett," his mum continued, her tone softening but no less earnest. "I don't think you should continue with this thing you have with her."

He sighed, his shoulders slumping. "Mum, just... I'll let her know when I think it's the right time," he said, his voice tinged with frustration. "We—she isn't ready for it right now. And I don't want to scare her away."

This was a conversation they had had too many times before. He had hoped for a quiet weekend with his mum, a brief reprieve before returning to Melbourne. But here they were again, circling the same issue.

"I'm just worried for you, is all," his mum said. Her words faltered, and she seemed to shrink in her seat. Ever since his dad had fallen ill, she had lost some of the quiet strength he had always associated with her.

Brett reached across the table and took her hands in his. They felt smaller than he remembered, frail even.

"I know, Mum. But I'll be fine," he said, trying to sound more confident than he felt. "And thanks for making dinner. It's delicious as usual."

A faint smile tugged at her lips. "So, eat more of it," she said, a hint of teasing in her voice.

He chuckled softly, the tension between them easing for a moment.

...———— ⚜ ————...

As Brett sat lost in his thoughts, the weight of indecision pressed heavily on his chest.

She meant *everything* to him, and the mere idea of losing her was unbearable. Yet, the truth he was hiding loomed like a storm cloud, threatening to shatter what they had built.

The irony wasn't lost on him: he had kept silent to protect her, but in doing so, he risked pushing her away.

His chest tightened as the realization set in.

The longer he buried the truth, the more damage he might cause.

She deserved his honesty, but how could he give her that when he wasn't sure they would survive it?

Brett exhaled shakily, his resolve wavering.

He couldn't ignore the gnawing fear that his silence—meant to shield her—might cost him the one person he wasn't ready to let go of.

Chapter Eleven: Facing Your Demons

Sheena replayed the conversation in her mind, dissecting every inflection, every pause, trying to make sense of what had happened.

It had been a couple of days since Alex had shown up unannounced at her place, stirring up emotions she thought she had buried long ago.

The kiss had been impulsive—a spark reignited that she hadn't even realized was still smouldering. She had brushed it off then, chalking it up to a fleeting moment of weakness. But now, it seemed Alex wasn't willing to let it go.

His words echoed in her head, refusing to fade.

"Sheena, you're not being fair," his voice had risen, tinged with exasperation. "You keep acting like I'm the one who walked away, but you're the one who kept shutting me out. Every time I got close, you pulled back."

His accusation had struck a nerve, though she had refused to let it show. "I'm not doing this, Alex. You made your choice when you decided to be with Natasha. Let's not rewrite history."

"Rewrite history?" he had snapped. "Are you serious? You pushed me away, Sheena! One minute, you were there, and the next, you were gone. Disappearing for weeks, sometimes months, like you didn't want to let me in. How was I supposed to fight for something you didn't even seem to want? Then came Natasha, and she knew exactly what she wanted. She made me feel needed. *You didn't.*"

Her stomach had twisted at his words. Had she really been the one to push him away? The idea unsettled her, but she couldn't let herself dwell on it.

"Alex, this isn't about blame. It's about moving on. And I have. You should, too."

The silence that had followed was deafening, thick with something unresolved. She could still hear the hurt in his voice as he finally said, "Maybe you're right. Maybe I should just let you go." He had ended the call abruptly, feeling frustrated with himself and with Sheena.

Now, in the stillness of her apartment, Sheena's mind raced. She stood near the dresser, her gaze flickering to the mirror. A strange reflection stared back at her. Her head felt heavy. The air felt heavy, suffocating, as if the walls were pressing in around her.

Her chest tightened as flashes of memory surfaced—unbidden, disjointed, like pieces of a puzzle she couldn't quite assemble.

The sound of shattering glass echoed in her ears, pulling her back to *that* moment at the café. The crash of the dropped tray had sent a wave of nausea rolling through her. She hadn't understood why at the time, but now, the edges of something dark and hidden began creeping into her consciousness.

She pressed her palms against her temples, willing the memories to stay buried.

But they wouldn't.

They pushed and clawed their way to the surface, fragments of a life she barely recognized.

Alex's voice from their argument surfaced again, but it wasn't about them this time.

"You told me you'd had an accident... but you never really talked about it. You were always so vague."

Sheena's breath hitched.

What accident?

A shiver ran down her spine.

She clenched her jaw, trying to focus, but the memories were relentless now.

A hospital room. The sterile smell of antiseptic. The faint beep of machines. The sound of muffled crying—her own? She couldn't be sure.

The memory was fleeting, blurred at the edges, yet it left her with an overwhelming sense of unease.

Sheena shook her head, trying to shake off the onslaught of emotion. She needed clarity. Answers.

But all she had were more questions.

Who was she, really? And why did it feel like the ground beneath her was crumbling, revealing a chasm she wasn't sure she could cross?

A sharp vibration against the wooden dresser snapped her back to the present. She turned her head, blinking at her phone's glowing screen.

A message from Alex. *I'm sorry. I didn't mean to hurt you or confuse you. I just... I wish I understood you better.*

Sheena stared at the words, her vision blurring with unshed tears.

She wanted to reply, to explain.

But what could she say when she didn't even understand herself?

Instead, she placed the phone down and sank to the floor, her back against the wall.

As she sat there, the shadows in the room seemed to deepen, stretching and twisting like the memories she couldn't quite grasp.

Somewhere in the distance, a clock chimed, its sound hollow and mournful.

Sheena closed her eyes, letting the darkness envelop her, the pieces of her fractured past pressing ever closer to the surface.

Part Three: Past Memories-Young Love or Something Like It

Chapter Twelve: The Carefree Days

The smell of cheap instant coffee and crumpled lecture notes filled the air of the shared student lounge. Sheena was perched on a rickety old couch, a pen tucked behind her ear as she flipped through the pages of her ethics textbook. Across from her, Alex was sprawled on the floor, lazily tossing a stress ball against the wall.

"You know," he mused, "we should just drop out and become full-time bartenders. Who needs a degree when you've got charm and an endless supply of bad jokes?"

Sheena snorted, not looking up from her notes. "You barely make enough tips to cover your instant noodles addiction. I don't think bartending is your golden ticket."

"I make enough to buy you a drink after exams," he countered, grinning. "That's got to count for something."

Their friendship had been effortless from the start— built on a shared love for dry humor, late-night debates over philosophy, and mutual enjoyment of late-night drives.

What had started as harmless flirtation over textbooks and shots at the pub had turned into something deeper, though neither of them had admitted it outright.

"Come on," Alex nudged her foot. "Put the book down for five minutes. Live a little."

She sighed, rolling her eyes but closing the textbook nonetheless. "Fine. But if I fail this class, I'm blaming you."

He smirked. "Deal. Now, what do you say to sneaking into the rooftop of the library? I hear the view's fantastic."

"Alex, that's literally trespassing."

"Only if we get caught."

She shook her head but stood anyway, grabbing her hoodie. "You're going to be the reason I have a criminal record one day."

"And what a great story that would be."

They climbed the fire escape, dodging campus security and laughing under their breath.

When they reached the rooftop, the entire city stretched out before them—lights twinkling against the ink-black sky. Sheena let out a breath she didn't realize she was holding.

"Wow."

Alex nudged her with his shoulder. "See? I have good ideas sometimes."

She turned to him, something unspoken passing between them. Maybe it was the adrenaline, or the way the moonlight softened the sharp angles of his face, but for the first time, she wondered what it would be like to let herself fall.

Sheena didn't believe in soulmates. But sitting there, shoulder to shoulder with Alex, she wondered if some connections were meant to exist before they even had a name.

Chapter Thirteen: France, 2003

It had only been a few weeks since her mother had stormed out of the house that evening, slamming the door behind her with a finality that left the walls trembling. That was when the cracks in her parents' marriage widened into gaping chasms.

Her father was always immersed in his work, his role as a diplomat pulling him in different directions. Late-night functions, overseas trips, and endless phone calls filled his days, making his presence at home feel fleeting. Though he was never truly gone, there were times when the house felt quieter without him—his absence lingering in the spaces he left behind.

Her mother, Abi, retaliated by carving out a life untethered to her husband or daughter. She filled the empty spaces with people Hannah didn't know—strangers who appeared in their home on weekends, bringing bottles of wine and boisterous laughter. The house would come alive with loud conversations and clinking glasses, but to Hannah, it felt no less lonely.

Sometimes, Abi would bring Hannah along to these parties, dressing her up in outfits far more extravagant than anything she was used to. She'd pull stylish pieces from boutiques Hannah had never even heard of, draping her in a world that felt both exciting and unfamiliar, slipping her into them with the precision of a stylist dressing a doll.

"You'll fit right in," her mother would chirp, but the clothes felt like costumes, as if Abi were trying to mould her into a different child—one who belonged in the world of exclusive soirées.

Some of the gatherings were unsettling in their predictability. The adults wore polished veneers, their smiles stretched too wide, and their words were perfunctory. They would nod at her, ask her polite questions, and then let their gazes drift away, already bored before she answered.

The other children were no kinder. Most avoided her altogether, turning her into a shadow lingering at the edges of the crowd. Some whispered behind their hands, casting sharp, cutting glances her way.

But there were exceptions—rare moments when she wasn't just a ghost floating unnoticed. And one of those exceptions was *Antoine*.

Hannah first met Antoine at one of the more lavish functions her mother dragged her to, hosted in a sprawling, glass-walled mansion that reeked of wealth and exclusivity. It was perched high on a hill, its manicured lawns sloping toward an infinity pool that seemed to spill into the horizon. The interior sparkled with crystal chandeliers and polished floors that reflected the dim glow of designer lighting.

The house belonged to Antoine's parents, and they were the kind of people who seemed larger than life. His father was a celebrated photographer, his quiet brilliance wrapped in an air of effortless sophistication.

Antoine's mother, a former model, carried herself with the poise of someone accustomed to admiration, her beauty only slightly softened by time and privilege.

Their family was untouchable in their perfection, their lives gliding smoothly along the surface of society's gaze.

Abi attended a charity event they hosted earlier in the year, and it seemed she had worked her way into their circle, securing invitations to subsequent events.

Her mother had been delighted by the invitation, practically buzzing with excitement as they arrived at the house.

"They're nice enough, I suppose," she later muttered to Hannah's father, rolling her eyes at their "pretentious" tastes in interior décor. Yet, at the party, she dripped with compliments and simpered her way through the evening, positioning herself in conversations with studied effort.

Hannah, however, had retreated to the farthest corner she could find, sketchpad in hand.

Drawing had become her refuge at events like this—something to do and focus on while the world carried on without her. She had been halfway through a rough sketch of the scene before her, trying to capture the chaos of clinking glasses and floating laughter, when a shadow fell across her page.

"*Enfin*! Someone here who shares my interests."

Startled, Hannah looked up into the face of a tall, lean boy with unruly curls and hazel eyes that seemed to see right through her. He was maybe seventeen, with an effortless charm and an easy smile. Beside him stood a girl with long blonde hair, sharp, angular features, and an expression of disinterest so pronounced it might as well have been painted on.

"Sorry?" Hannah managed.

"I said, I'm glad someone else finds this kind of event boring enough to sketch." He gestured toward her sketch with genuine curiosity. "May I?"

Reluctantly, she held up her sketchpad.

"You're good," he said, and it didn't sound like flattery. "I'm Antoine. And this," he gestured dismissively to the blonde girl clinging to his arm, "is Monique. She doesn't share our art appreciation, sadly."

Monique's rouge-tinted lips twisted into a lazy smile, as though to prove she didn't care. "*Salut*," she said flatly.

Antoine seemed unfazed. "Do you mind?" he asked, tilting his head toward her sketch. "Can I show you something?"

Before she could answer, he motioned for her to follow him.

Curiosity won over hesitation, and Hannah found herself trailing Antoine up a winding staircase to a bedroom that was easily twice the size of hers. It was immaculate—surprisingly so for a teenage boy—and smelled faintly of cologne, fresh linen, and a hint of tobacco. The walls were decorated with framed French art and black-and-white photos—moody shots of canals, alleyways, and foggy landscapes. Hannah guessed they were his father's work.

Antoine crossed the room and retrieved a leather-bound journal from his desk, holding it out to her with quiet pride.

"These are mine."

Hannah leafed through the pages, her fingers tracing the intricate pencil strokes—detailed landscapes, still life, even a few portraits. The sketches were vivid, almost alive, as though they might leap off the page. She looked up at him, genuinely impressed.

"These are beautiful," she said softly.

"Merci," he said, sitting down on the edge of a chaise longue opposite her. "What inspires you to draw?"

Hannah hesitated, caught off guard by the question. "I don't know," she said finally. "I guess it helps me feel... less invisible."

Antoine studied her for a long moment, his hazel eyes softening.

"You're not invisible," he said simply.

From across the room, Monique let out a shrill laugh into her mobile phone, her French spilling out in fast, clipped sentences as she flipped through a copy of a *CosmoGirl* magazine with the photo of Angelina Jolie on the front cover. After a beat, she got up, muttering something about getting another drink, and slammed the door behind her on the way out.

The silence that followed felt heavier than before.

"I hope I didn't upset her," Hannah murmured, suddenly feeling self-conscious.

Antoine waved it off with an easy shrug. "She's fine. Monique gets bored easily."

He leaned forward, his gaze flickering over her face with a quiet intensity.

"You know, I'd love to draw you."

Hannah blinked. "Me?"

"Yes. You have interesting features—very textured," he said, as though cataloguing the angles of her face. "You'd make an amazing subject."

Hannah blushed, dropping her eyes to the journal still in her lap. "I don't know... I'm sure Monique would make a better model."

Antoine laughed softly, shaking his head. "Monique is too vain for that. Her beauty's a dime a dozen—obvious and fleeting. You... you're something different."

Hannah gulped, feeling her cheeks flush deeper. "Perhaps another time," she managed. "But I should go now. My mum will be looking for me." It wasn't entirely true—her mother was probably three glasses of champagne in and wouldn't notice her absence—but she needed an exit.

Antoine stood and opened the door for her. "If you change your mind, come to my birthday party. It's in a few weeks."

He pressed a scrap of paper with his number into her hand.

"It's my eighteenth," he said, grinning. "I'd love to see you there."

Hannah nodded, clutching the paper tightly as she slipped past him.

As she descended the staircase, the party noise swelled around her again—laughter, music, the clink of glass—and yet she felt oddly distant from it all, as though part of her were still back in that room, surrounded by the faint scent of cologne, sketches, and the lingering memory of hazel eyes.

Chapter Fourteen: Ma Petite

"You can't wear that!" Hannah's mother exclaimed, yanking a plain white blouse and jeans from her daughter's wardrobe with obvious disapproval.

"It looks too... ordinary. Don't you have anything more chic and elegant?" Her manicured fingers flitted through the hangers like a bird pecking for something better.

Hannah resisted the urge to roll her eyes. "Mum, it's just a party. I don't think it really matters." She sighed, already regretting saying yes to this. A small part of her was curious about how the night would unfold, but not enough to justify the ordeal of a fashion intervention by her mum.

Her mother dismissed her protest with a wave of her hand. "Better to be overdressed than underdressed, *ma petite*," she declared, using the same patronizing nickname she always did when grooming Hannah like one of her charity projects.

Within the hour, Hannah found herself at the mall, trailing behind her mother, who attacked the shopping trip with military precision: a sequined mini skirt, a halter-neck top, and a dark blue leather jacket. Each choice was made with the kind of confidence that brooked no argument.

Hannah hesitated as she looked at her reflection under the dressing room lights, feeling like she was slipping into someone else's skin. She didn't recognize herself. But her mum was already ringing up the purchase.

"These are *party* clothes, darling," she said dismissively when Hannah suggested something simpler. "You'll thank me later."

Surprisingly, the night turned out better than she had expected. She had braced herself for a gathering of pretentious, overindulged teens, but Antoine's party was more intimate, his friends refreshingly friendly. Monique was there, of course, but she seemed preoccupied, her attention divided among others in the room.

The party settled into an easy rhythm of conversation and music as the spacious loft transformed into a youthful haven adorned with string lights, eclectic posters, and splashes of neon. The air vibrated with the pulsing beats of Daft Punk's *"One More Time"* alongside the irresistible pop of Alizée's *"Moi... Lolita,"* setting an upbeat tone.

Hannah kept herself occupied with the elaborate trays of canapés and non-alcoholic drinks, savouring smoked salmon blinis and miniature éclairs while politely declining offers of wine and champagne. Her mother would sniff it out on her breath in an instant.

As the party settled into an easy rhythm of conversation and music, Antoine began opening his gifts. A knot tightened in Hannah's stomach as he reached for hers.

What could you possibly give someone like Antoine—a rich kid with a famous photographer for a father and a former model for a mother? She had agonized over the question before finally deciding to recreate the sketch she had been working on the night they met.

Encased in an acrylic box frame, the drawing was an abstract depiction of a hummingbird and a flower. The bird pulsed with life, its fragmented wings creating an illusion of movement, while the flower unfurled in dreamlike spirals, its lines interwoven with energy. Dots and swirls filled the negative space, capturing the hum of wings and the scatter of pollen.

Antoine's face lit up as he pulled it from the wrapping.

"I *love* it," he said, his grin boyish, disarming. He held it up for everyone to see. "This is going on my wall."

His friends murmured compliments, some nodding in admiration. Monique, however, merely smirked, her lips curling into something between amusement and condescension.

"How charming," she said, her voice saccharine with insincerity.

But Antoine ignored her, turning to Hannah. "It's incredible," he said, hazel eyes locking onto hers. "Seriously, thank you."

A blush crept up her cheeks. "I'm glad you like it," she murmured, tucking a stray curl behind her ear.

Later, as the party wound down and plans were made to head to a club, Hannah called her mum to pick her up. Most of Antoine's friends were over eighteen, and she had no interest in trying to talk her way into a venue where she wasn't welcome.

As she stood near the entrance, Antoine came to see her off.

"Thanks for coming," he said, hands buried in the pockets of his tailored blazer. "You're cool to hang out with—not many people want to talk about art at these things."

Hannah smiled. "I enjoyed it. Thanks for inviting me."

He hesitated, then grinned. "So... what about that sketch of you? I keep thinking about it." His voice had that teasing yet earnest quality that made her pulse quicken.

She shifted slightly. "I'd have to ask my parents." She tried to sound nonchalant, though she knew her mother would encourage it while her father—if he even noticed—might have questions.

Antoine raised an eyebrow, his grin widening. "Just tell them you're hanging out with me and my friends if they're worried about you being alone with a strange older guy, *n'est-ce pas?*"

"You're not *that* much older than me," she said, feeling bold. "I'll be sixteen real soon."

"*Ah, très bien!* You're practically grown-up, then." His smirk was playful, but his gaze was intent.

Something about the moment emboldened her. "Maybe I'll take you up on that offer. Let's see what you've got."

Antoine's grin spread, his eyes gleaming with satisfaction. "*C'est ça!* You've made my day! I'll call you later this week to set something up."

As she leaned in to kiss him on the cheek before leaving, she caught Monique's gaze from across the room—sharp, watchful, resentful.

For a brief moment, Hannah felt a flicker of triumph.

But as she stepped outside into the crisp night air, the elation faded, replaced by something heavier, more uncertain.

She couldn't shake the feeling that this budding friendship with Antoine would bring complications for which she wasn't prepared.

Part Four:

Past and Present Explained

Chapter Fifteen: May Day

Lola had been trying to reach Sheena all morning, but her calls kept going unanswered. The night they had spent together was still fresh in her mind—a tentative evening of guarded conversation, where they had danced around revealing too much about themselves. Yet, despite the caution, it had felt surprisingly... nice. A connection she hadn't expected.

"So, are we friends now?" Lola had asked, half-joking as she stood outside, waiting for her Uber.

"Don't push it," Sheena had replied with a cheeky smile, her tone teasing but her eyes distant. "I still don't know how I feel about you contacting me out of the blue. But..." She paused, as though carefully choosing her next words, "I think some of the answers you're looking for might be better found on your own. Sometimes, it's better to let the past stay in the past. That's my approach, anyway."

Lola had opened her mouth to protest, but Sheena held up a hand. "No more questions about Brett's ex. Trust yourself and maybe trust him too. Or..." Sheena shrugged; her gaze fixed on the dim glow of a nearby streetlamp. "You could let him go. Give yourself a chance to forge another life elsewhere—with someone else, maybe."

The words had stung, but before Lola could process them, Sheena had shifted her weight and added, "But do the bloody test already."

Lola blinked at her, taken aback by the sudden bluntness.

Sheena had sighed, her voice softening. "I know it's terrifying. Especially when you don't have many people to lean on. But if it turns out to be... you know, positive, and you feel like you need to talk about it, you can call me." Sheena's tone was casual, almost nonchalant, but the offer had landed heavily on Lola's chest.

Lola had nodded, emotions rising unexpectedly. "Thanks, Sheena. That means a lot." She had wiped at the tear threatening to spill from the corner of her eye, embarrassed by her sudden vulnerability.

They had stood in silence after that, an unspoken understanding passing between them until the hum of Lola's Uber pulling up broke the stillness. As the car arrived, she had given Sheena a small, awkward wave.

"Good luck," Sheena had said, nodding with a faint smile.

The car had turned a corner, taking Lola home but also leaving her with a sense of something unfinished.

Now, sitting in her apartment, Lola sighed as she stared at her phone. Sheena was still unresponsive. Maybe she had expected too much. Maybe the brief connection they'd shared hadn't meant as much to Sheena as it had to her.

Lola's thoughts drifted to her best friend in America, Ona. Ona had always been her go-to in times of crisis, the one person she felt who would never judge her and always knew what to say. Lately, however, Lola had felt a reluctance to reach out to her.

Another sigh escaped her lips as her eyes moved to the phone screen again. *Missed Calls: Brett (3)* stared back at her. She felt a pang of guilt and frustration. She had been avoiding his calls for days, unable to face him until she figured out what she wanted—or, more accurately, what she needed.

It was time. Time to stop running. Time to decide.

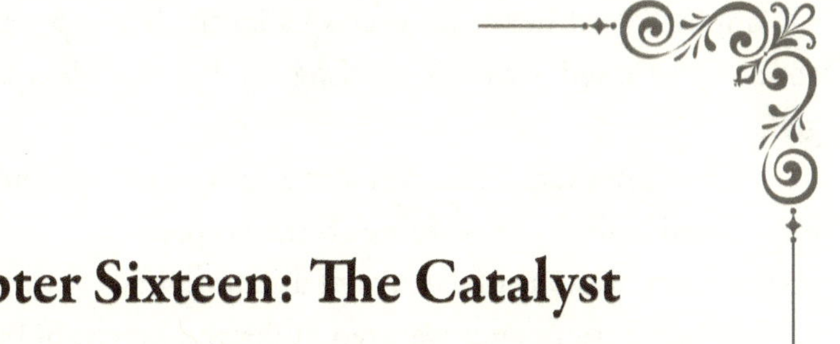

Chapter Sixteen: The Catalyst

Hannah stood on the doorstep, the cold evening air biting at her cheeks and seeping through her coat. The faint glow of the porch light above cast her shadow long and unsteady against the gravel driveway. Her breath curled in soft clouds before her, but it did little to calm the storm raging inside.

She had rehearsed this moment over and over again, pacing her room, whispering the words into the empty space, willing herself to sound calm and collected.

But now, with her heart pounding like a war drum, she felt small and unprepared. She had picked herself up from a week of sleepless nights and swollen eyes to be here. And now, standing on this threshold, doubt began to gnaw at her resolve.

When her parents had asked where she was going, she told them that she was going to see a movie with a friend from school.

Maybe this was a mistake. Maybe she should just walk away.

Before she could decide, the door creaked open, and the decision was made for her. Hannah's stomach twisted. It wasn't Antoine who answered but his mother, Sophie Delacroix.

The woman was as stunning and intimidating as Hannah remembered.

Sophie's statuesque frame, impeccably tailored silk blouse, and effortlessly sharp gaze belonged to someone who commanded rooms with her presence alone. She wasn't just a former model turned business mogul—she was a force of nature, and Hannah suddenly felt like a misplaced leaf caught in her draft.

"*Peux-je vous aider?*" Sophie asked, her tone clipped, her blue eyes narrowing as they studied Hannah.

Hannah fidgeted, fumbling for composure. "*B-Bon nuit*. I'm... Hannah," she stammered. "I was hoping to, um, speak with Antoine?"

Sophie tilted her head ever so slightly, her expression impassive. "What about?" she asked, switching to English, her voice low and smooth but cold as glass.

Hannah hesitated. She was sure Sophie must remember her. They had been introduced before—at Antoine's birthday party, at least briefly. But the look on Sophie's face was one of calculated unfamiliarity.

Hannah's confidence wavered under the weight of her gaze.

"I... It's ... personal," Hannah managed. "I just need a moment of his time."

Sophie's perfectly arched brow lifted in a gesture that was somehow both sceptical and dismissive.

"Antoine is busy, and this is not a good time. You should call before coming unannounced. That is the proper thing to do," she said, each word clipped and precise.

"I understand," Hannah said quickly, "but it's urgent. Please, if you could just—"

Sophie silenced her with a raised hand, her polished nails gleaming in the porch light. "What is your name again?"

"Hannah," she repeated, her voice faltering.

A moment of silence passed between them, the kind that stretched thin and taut. Then Sophie's expression hardened.

"Ah, Hannah. Yes, I know who you are," Sophie said, her tone sharp enough to slice. "Antoine has already told me about... your claims. Let me make this very clear. I will not tolerate baseless accusations against my son. I know *your type*." Her words dripped with disdain.

"You think you can exploit our kindness, leverage proximity to our family for your own gain, but you are mistaken. Do not come here again. *Comprenez-vous?*"

Hannah's heart plummeted, her breath catching in her throat. "I—I'm not like that, and I'm not lying," she protested weakly, but Sophie had already turned away.

Before Hannah could say more, the door slammed shut with a resounding finality that echoed in the quiet street. She stood there, stunned, the words she had so carefully rehearsed crumbling into nothing.

As she turned to leave, her shoulders hunched against the chill, she felt the prickling sensation of being watched. She glanced up and saw a figure framed in the upstairs window—Monique.

She stood there, her face etched with disdain, her arms crossed as she looked down at Hannah like she was something unpleasant stuck to her shoe.

Then another figure appeared behind her—Antoine. His expression was pained, his hand resting hesitantly on the windowsill. Hope sparked in Hannah's chest, only to be extinguished when Monique leaned close, whispering something to him. She touched his shoulder, her fingers lingering, and turned him away from the window.

Hannah stood frozen on the spot, staring up at the darkened glass. Whatever words she had left dissolved into the icy night air. Finally, she turned and walked back down the driveway, the sound of her footsteps swallowed by the encroaching shadows.

…——— ⚜ ———…

There was a gentle knock on the door. Hannah's heart gave a slight startle. It was her dad. He opened the door of her room a crack and peered through. "Is it safe to come in?" he asked, his voice soft and careful. She hesitated for a moment, then nodded, pulling her knees closer as she sat cross-legged on her bed. Her CD player was still in her lap, Dido's *No Angel* humming faintly in her ears until she took the headphones out.

Her dad stepped in, smiling a little, though the corners of his mouth twitched with fatigue.

"How are you doing, kiddo? I feel like I haven't seen you in a while. You're growing up so fast before my very eyes," he said, sitting gingerly on the edge of her bed.

His wry smile couldn't hide the exhaustion etched on his face. Dark circles under his eyes told the story of jet lag and lengthy meetings. He'd only returned from an overseas trip a few days ago, yet work had already consumed him.

Hannah managed a tight smile. "How was your trip?" she asked, her voice light but distant.

"Hectic," he groaned, rubbing his temples. "Traveling is not as great as people make it out to be. And I always wish I was here with you instead," he added gently.

But you aren't, Hannah thought. She swallowed her bitterness and said, "Maybe you should trade places with Mum, then. She makes it seem like you're out there having the time of your life while we're here."

Her dad raised his eyebrows, his lips twitching into a knowing smirk. "Of course she does," he said, leaning back slightly. "But I have a feeling she wouldn't be too impressed with hours on a plane only to spend days in boardrooms arguing over contracts with people who don't even like you." He chuckled, shaking his head.

"Anyway, how are things with you?" he asked, his tone softening. "How was the movie last night? Your mum said you went with a friend from school?"

Hannah's stomach churned. She hated lying, especially to her dad. But she couldn't bring herself to tell him the truth. A lump formed in her throat, and her voice trembled slightly as she said, "Yeah, it was okay."

"What did you see?"

"*Pirates of the Caribbean*," she replied quickly, surprised at how smoothly the lie slipped out. She glanced at the posters on her wall for validation, as if they'd justify her words. It *was* a movie she wanted to see, and her friends at school had been buzzing about it.

Her dad nodded thoughtfully. "Did you have a good time, *me hearty*?" he asked in a mock sailor's accent.

She nodded again, her gaze fixed on the patterned quilt beneath her. The images from last week flashed unbidden before her eyes. All she wanted to do was scream, but the words lodged deep in her throat like a stone.

"Well, how about you and your old man go see a movie sometime next week?" he offered, his voice warm. "Your pick. I miss hanging out with you."

Hannah's heart ached at his kindness, but her lips stayed pressed into a thin line.

"Are you sure everything's okay, Hannah?" he asked, his brow furrowing with concern.

She forced herself to meet his gaze. "Yeah, I'm fine, dad. I just... I've had a headache. Didn't sleep well last night," she murmured. It wasn't entirely a lie, but it wasn't the truth either.

"Oh, Hannah," he said, his voice heavy with concern. "You should've told us earlier. You're not overworking yourself, are you? Is something bothering you?" His worry deepened, etched into the lines of his forehead.

Hannah shook her head quickly and bit her tongue. *Don't say anything. It'll just make everything worse.*

"All right," he sighed, standing up. "I'll grab you some pain relief tablets. Try to get some proper rest tonight, okay?"

He hesitated before adding, "I'll ask Mum to check in on you. She's trying to figure out where she wants us to go for her birthday dinner tomorrow."

The birthday dinner was a blur. Hannah moved through the day like an automaton, her mind foggy and her heart heavy.

At school, she struggled to focus as the vivid, haunting images from last week—of Antoine's room, his unrelenting hands—played relentlessly in her mind. By midday, she asked to leave early, citing exhaustion.

At home that evening, her mum's sharp gaze fell on her. "So, what's up, Hannah?" she asked, crossing her arms.

"You've been a real sourpuss this week. And don't tell me you're unwell. You're not feverish, you're not sniffly... I *know* when you're sick," she said matter-of-factly.

"Your dad's worried. So am I. If something's on your mind, it's better to let it out than to bottle it all in."

Her mum's eyes softened, and something in her tone broke through Hannah's defences.

The words tumbled out before she could stop them. "Mum... he forced himself on me. I didn't want to. I didn't..." Her voice cracked, and the tears came, fast and heavy. Her chest heaved as the memories overwhelmed her. She felt her breath quicken, her mind spiralling back to that night.

It had started so innocently. His friends had been over for a while, but they'd left early. Monique wasn't there. She'd thought nothing of it as Antoine handed her the finished sketch he'd drawn of her. "I wanted to wait until they were gone to show you this," he'd said softly.

"Wow, Antoine," she'd whispered, awestruck. "This is beautiful. I... I look beautiful."

"That's because you are... *Tu es tres belle.*" He was looking at her intently. She looked down, too shy to look up at him.

She hadn't noticed how close he was sitting until his hand gently tilted her chin upward. His lips were on hers before she'd processed what was happening.

It wasn't entirely unwelcome, not at first. But then his kiss grew harder, his hands rough, groping, and insistent. She froze. *What was happening now*? This wasn't what she wanted.

She felt herself putting a hand on his shoulder to signal she was not interested in going ahead, but he did not even notice this and instead pushed her down on the bed; he was breathing fast and making a weird grunting noise; she was now very scared. She felt suffocated - trapped.

Her voice, weak and trembling, couldn't reach him.

"Antoine, please..." she'd pleaded, but he wasn't listening. It was like he had become possessed. He'd become someone she didn't recognize. *Antoine* was no longer Antoine. She couldn't make sense of what was happening. It was all too much.

Panic had set in, and she'd frozen, retreating into herself as her body stopped resisting and her mind floated above the scene, detached and numb.

...———⚜———...

Back in the present, Hannah's sobs filled the room. Her mum sat stunned, her face pale. "What?! Antoine Delacroix?" she asked, her voice barely above a whisper.

When Hannah nodded, her mum's hands clenched into fists. "I... I don't understand. You mean he..." She couldn't finish the sentence, as though saying the words would make them unbearably real.

Hannah nodded mutely, her mum a soft blur through the tears that clouded her eyes. Her breathing was uneven, her chest heaving as if trying to draw in more air than her lungs could hold.

"Okay, just breathe, sweetie," her mum said gently, her voice a fragile thread of calm. She reached for Hannah's trembling hands, squeezing them with a reassuring firmness. "I'll get you some water, alright? Don't move. I'll be right back."

Hannah nodded again, but her gaze remained fixed on the floor, her body frozen in a tight coil of tension. The sound of her mum's retreating footsteps echoed faintly down the hallway.

When her mum returned, she had a tray in her hands with a glass of water and a mug of steaming cocoa. She set them down carefully on Hannah's bedside table. "Here you go, honey. Try to drink a little—it'll help."

Hannah managed a small sip of water, but the cocoa went untouched. The warm, sweet scent filled the room, but she couldn't bring herself to lift the mug. Her mum sat beside her, rubbing small circles on her back, her touch both soothing and grounding.

"It's okay," her mum murmured. "You don't have to say anything more tonight. Just rest."

Hannah felt her mum press a small pill into her hand at some point. "This will help you sleep, sweetheart. You need it."

Hannah swallowed it obediently, too drained to resist. Soon after, she felt her body surrender to exhaustion, slipping into a dreamless void.

...——— ⚜ ———...

The following day, Hannah stirred awake, her head heavy and her thoughts sluggish. The sunlight filtered through her curtains in thin, muted beams, casting a pale golden glow across her room. She blinked against the brightness, her mind sluggishly piecing together the previous night's events.

Her door cracked open without warning, and her mum appeared, holding a laundry basket. "Oh, good, you're awake," she said, her voice brisk but soft.

"I've been in a few times, but you were out cold. Your dad wanted to say goodbye before he left, but I told him you needed the rest."

She crossed the room, pulling back the curtains with a practised swish. "How are you feeling today?"

Hannah sat up slowly, her body heavy with the grogginess that lingered like a fog. "I think I'm okay," she mumbled, stifling a yawn. "The sleep helped a bit, but I feel... weird. What did you give me?"

"A relaxant," her mum said simply, adjusting the edge of the curtains. "You were very wound-up last night. You needed it."

The mention of last night made Hannah's stomach lurch. She bit her lower lip, the sharp sting reminding her of the bruising from Antoine's bite. She winced and pressed her lips together tightly, willing the memory to retreat.

"Why don't you have a warm shower?" her mum suggested. "It'll help clear your head. Breakfast is ready when you're done. I called your school and told them you're unwell, so you're staying home today."

Downstairs, the kitchen smelled faintly of butter and sugar. Crepes, Hannah realized, her heart twisting painfully. It used to be her favourite breakfast, but today, the sight of the delicate stack on her plate made her stomach churn.

"You need to eat," her mum said, sipping her black coffee and spreading radish slices on crusty bread. Her sharp gaze darted to Hannah, who was listlessly pushing the crepes around her plate with a fork.

"I'm not hungry," Hannah murmured, barely audible.

"You have to try," her mum pressed, her tone soft but firm. "We need to talk about last night, *ma petite*."

Hannah flinched at the pet name. It grated against her raw nerves, a term of endearment that felt out of place after everything that had happened.

Her mum's expression didn't waver. "Your dad asked about you before he left. I told him you were unwell. It's a good thing he's away for a couple of days—he'd know something was wrong."

She paused, clasping her hands around her coffee mug. "Here's what I think we should do," she said, her voice adopting a deliberate tone. "We shouldn't tell him anything. It'll upset him greatly."

The words hit Hannah like a slap. "Upset him?" she repeated, her voice cracking. A surge of anger bubbled to the surface, breaking through her numbness. "He is my dad! He *should* be upset, Mum! I was—"

"Stop it, Hannah," her mum interrupted sharply, her own voice rising. "Stop throwing around wild accusations. Do you even understand what this could do? To your dad? His diplomatic career? To you?"

Hannah's breath hitched, her eyes widening in disbelief.

"You'll ruin so many opportunities for yourself, Hannah," her mum continued, her tone shifting to something colder, more calculated. "And you'll bring stigma on yourself that you might never escape."

"Mum, he *raped* me," Hannah whispered, her voice trembling. The words felt jagged, raw, and unreal, slicing through the air between them.

Her mum's expression tightened, flinching at the word. "Hannah, listen to me. I'm not saying it wasn't upsetting, but... are you sure you're remembering things correctly?"

Abi gave a deep sigh, her tone softening slightly. "Maybe I should've had this conversation with you sooner. These things happen, you know. Sometimes, what starts as something mutual can feel different afterwards. Maybe... you just regretted it later?"

Hannah stared at her, the air in the room thick and suffocating. Her mother's words were muffled and distant, as if spoken from underwater.

"We need to be practical," her mum said. First, we need to take a test."

"A test?" Hannah echoed, her voice faint.

"Yes. A pregnancy test. Just to be sure."

Her mum's words swirled around her, nonsensical and surreal. "I can't be. I *can't*—" Hannah stammered, her vision blurring as her breath quickened.

The last thing she saw was her untouched plate of crepes before the world tilted, and everything went dark.

Chapter Seventeen: Gareth – September 2011

Brett sat at the kitchen table, absently running his finger along the rim of his coffee cup. The house was still, save for the quiet hum of the ceiling fan and the faint beeping of the blood pressure monitor his father had started using with increasing regularity.

His father shuffled into the kitchen, moving with the careful slowness of someone who had been awake for hours. He lowered himself into the chair across from Brett, exhaling as he leaned back.

"Couldn't sleep again?" Brett asked, glancing up.

His father shook his head, rubbing a hand over his face. "Not for long. No point lying there staring at the ceiling."

Brett nodded, taking a sip of his coffee.

"How's work?" his father asked after a pause, his voice rough with sleep—or maybe something deeper.

"Busy. Same old stuff," Brett replied, the familiar answer coming easily.

His father gave a slow nod, his gaze fixed on the tabletop. "That's good. Keeping busy keeps the mind sharp."

There was something in the way he said it, as if reminding himself just as much as he was advising Brett.

Brett wanted to say something more—something that would bridge the growing distance between them—but the words felt too big to fit between the walls of this house. Instead, he studied the pill bottles lining the counter.

"They say the high blood pressure's under control now," his father said, following Brett's gaze. "The dizziness. The headaches. The... moments where my body just won't listen. But I'm feeling ok today."

Brett's throat tightened. He had been reading up on it—hypertension leading to strokes, how it could creep up on someone without warning.

He had seen the way his father's hands sometimes trembled when he reached for his glass, how his gait had slowed over the past year.

"You need to take it easy, Dad", Brett finally said.

Brett's father exhaled sharply, shaking his head. "And let this house fall apart? You know that's not happening."

Brett leaned back, arms crossed, watching as his father rubbed absently at his knee—one of the many aches he rarely acknowledged.

"I just need to fix a few things," his father continued, his voice laced with stubborn determination. "The fence out back is barely standing, and the gutters need clearing before the next big rain. And don't get me started on that damn creaky floorboard in the hallway."

Brett sighed. "Dad, that's exactly what I mean. You don't have to do it all yourself. Just let me or Mum get someone in."

His father waved a dismissive hand. "I don't need anyone coming in to do what I can still do myself."

Brett studied him—the slight tremor in his fingers and exhaustion lingering beneath the surface. His father had always been a man of action, taking pride in keeping things in order and being practical. Slowing down wasn't in his nature, no matter what his body was trying to tell him.

"Just... promise me you won't push yourself too hard," Brett said, his voice softer now.

His father gave him a slight, knowing smirk. "I'll take it easy when the house stops needing me."

Brett didn't push the argument further. They both knew his father wasn't going to stop anytime soon.

There was a flicker of something unreadable in his father's eyes. Maybe pride. Maybe regret. He tapped his fingers against the table, the small tremor more noticeable than before.

"You're a good son, but you need to stop treating me like I'm bloody dying." his father said quietly.

Brett sighed, forcing a small smile. "And you're a stubborn old man."

His father chuckled, shaking his head. "Runs in the family."

A silence settled between them—not heavy, but familiar. Brett tried not to let his worry show, but it was there, lurking beneath the surface.

His father had always been strong and steady, someone who never let anything shake him. But now, Brett could see the cracks forming, the slow unravelling of the man that had always seemed larger than life.

The sound of rain pattered softly against the window. Brett reached for the deck of cards on the counter, holding them up with a small grin. "Fancy losing another round of poker?"

His father smirked, reaching out with his slightly unsteady hand. "Only if you're ready to lose your money."

As they played, the world outside faded away, the weight of unspoken worries momentarily forgotten—for a little while, before everything shifted, before life moved forward in ways neither of them could predict.

Chapter Eighteen: The Great Revelation (2024)

Lola pressed her forehead against the cool glass of the taxi window, watching the city blur past in a streak of neon and shadow. Her stomach twisted with nerves, a churning mix of anxiety and reluctant anticipation. Brett had called her earlier, and she had answered for the first time in weeks. His voice had been quiet but steady, tinged with something close to urgency.

"Just come over," he had said. *"I need to show you something."*

So here she was, pulled by an invisible thread she didn't quite understand. She had spent so long running from the truth and herself, but she would face it tonight.

When the taxi pulled up outside Brett's apartment, she hesitated for only a second before stepping out into the night air. The weight in her chest didn't ease as she made her way up the stairs.

Brett answered the door before she had a chance to knock. He stepped aside silently, letting her in. His expression was unreadable, but there was something in his eyes—concern, maybe even regret. He lingered for a moment before murmuring, "Make yourself comfortable. I just need to take a call."

And then he was gone, leaving her alone in the stillness of his apartment.

Lola gave a slow sigh, rubbing her arms as she stepped toward the kitchen. Her mouth was dry, and she needed something—water, maybe just a moment to breathe. She pulled open a cupboard, searching for a glass, when her eyes landed on a box sitting on the kitchen table.

It was old, the cardboard was worn at the edges, and the lid was slightly ajar. A strange unease settled over her as she stepped closer.

Inside, a mix of belongings lay stacked haphazardly—some clothes, faded photographs, a battered sketchbook, and, at the very top, a journal.

Lola hesitated, her fingertips grazing the leather cover. Something about it made her pulse quicken. Slowly, she lifted it from the box and opened it to the first page.

The handwriting was hers. Or at least—it looked like hers. But the words felt unfamiliar, as if someone else had written them.

The entries varied—some light and playful, others dark, heavy with despair. The handwriting shifted subtly from one page to the next, as if different versions of herself had taken turns chronicling her life. One passage stood out:

I saw her again today. When our reflections met in the mirror, she felt like a stranger. Who is she? And who have I become?

Lola's hands trembled as she flipped through more pages. Sketches filled the spaces between the words—faces she didn't recognize.

One in particular made her stomach tighten: a child's face, angelic and serene, with the name "Chrissie" scrawled beneath it. A wave of nausea rolled through her, her pulse hammering in her ears.

"Lola?"

She flinched at the sound of Brett's voice. He stood in the doorway, his face lined with concern.

She held up the journal. "What is this, Brett? These aren't all my words. Why do I have this?"

Brett exhaled, stepping toward her. "Because you kept it," he said quietly. "Back when you lived here."

Her throat tightened. "Lived here?"

"You don't remember, do you?" His voice was heavy, laced with something close to sorrow. "You weren't just Lola then. You were Sheena. And before that, Hannah."

A cold wave of confusion washed over her. "What are you talking about?"

"You've been... dissociating," he said softly. "For years. After what happened when you were younger. Antoine. The trauma of losing Chrissie... It was too much for you to handle, so your mind created other versions of you to protect you."

She stared at him, her vision swimming. "No. No, that doesn't make sense. I would know if... if I wasn't..." Her voice faltered.

"You don't remember because that's how dissociation works," Brett explained, his voice breaking. "Sheena is your fearless, adventurous side.

Hannah is the part of you that couldn't cope after Chrissie. And you, Lola... you're the one holding everything together right now."

There was a tightness in her chest as memories began to surface—memories she hadn't even realized were buried. She saw herself as a teenager, sketching in Antoine's room while Monique glared from the corner. She saw herself pleading with her mother to believe her after Antoine had assaulted her, only to be met with cold denial. She saw herself in a hospital bed, her body wracked with sobs as doctors murmured empty consolations.

And then—

The phone call.

It had been a warm afternoon. She remembered staring at her phone screen, Brett's name flashing across it. She had almost let it go to voicemail. Almost.

But something in her had answered.

His voice had been frantic, broken. *"Chrissie... she—she's gone, Hannah. She's gone. Dad took her into the water, and then he had a stroke. He -"*

Her knees had buckled beneath her.

She hadn't been *there*. She hadn't seen *it* happen. But the devastation, the loss—it had consumed her just the same.

The weight of the memory sent a fresh wave of nausea through her. She clutched the edge of the table, the journal slipping from her grasp, falling to the floor with a dull thud.

"Chrissie," she whispered, the name like a razor against her throat. The weight of it crushed her, suffocating and unrelenting.

Before she could move, Brett was there.

He stepped forward quickly, crouching beside her as the journal lay between them. "Hannah..." His voice was softer now, cautious. Referring to her by that name felt strange - foreign yet very familiar to Lola. He reached out, but hesitated, as if unsure whether she would let him touch her.

Brett knelt in front of her, his hands warm against her knees. "You loved her so much. And losing her... it shattered you. But you're stronger than you know. You've survived this long. And now you're starting to remember."

She shook her head, pressing a hand against her chest, trying to steady her breathing. "I... I don't understand," she whispered.

A shuddering breath escaped her as she whispered, "I don't know who I am anymore."

She shook her head, sobbing. "Why didn't you tell me? Why did you keep this from me?"

"Because I didn't want to hurt you more than you've already been hurt," he admitted, his voice thick with emotion. "I thought if I could help you heal without forcing you to face it all at once... maybe you'd be okay. But I see now that you need to know. You deserve the truth."

The room tilted as she tried to process everything. Her hands clutched the journal. It felt like she was fracturing, shattering into pieces too small to put back together. And yet, at the same time, something inside her was aligning, clicking into place.

She saw Hannah's laughter, Sheena's defiance, and her own quiet resilience. They weren't separate anymore. They were her.

"I don't know if I can do this," she whispered.

Brett took her hands in his, steadying her. "You can. And I'll be here every step of the way."

For the first time in a long time, Lola felt the weight of her fractured past begin to lift. It would take time to heal, to piece together the life she thought she knew. But for now, she let herself lean into Brett's embrace, holding onto the fragile hope that maybe, just maybe, she could find wholeness again.

"There's something else you should know," Brett said, his voice hesitant. Her heart skipped a beat. She didn't know if she could handle any more revelations.

She stilled herself as he met her gaze.

"I called your dad and told him everything."

Chapter Nineteen: The Path to Healing

Dr Evelyn Hartley glanced at her notes before looking back at Hannah. "It's been almost a year since you last came in," she said gently. "What made you decide to return?"

Hannah hesitated, her fingers tightening slightly in her lap. She had expected this question, but answering it still felt like exposing something raw. "I guess... things started slipping again," she admitted.

"The dreams, the vague thoughts, the confusion, feeling like I'm watching my life instead of living it." She let out a shaky breath. "And Sheena's been showing up more."

Evelyn nodded, her expression calm and patient. "That makes sense. When stress, trauma, or unresolved emotions resurface, dissociation can become more pronounced. Sometimes, parts of us step forward to cope in ways we might not even recognize."

Hannah swallowed. "Yeah... I thought maybe I had it under control. But I – I don't."

Dr. Hartley studied her. "Coming back is a big step, Hannah. A brave one. And it means you're ready to understand more—about yourself, your alters, and why they're here."

Hannah let the words settle. The truth was, she wasn't sure if she was *ready*—but she was here. And maybe that was enough.

Evelyn adjusted her glasses as she regarded the young woman across from her. "Tell me about Sheena and Lola again," she prompted gently.

The woman shifted on the couch, fingers twisting in her lap. "Sheena is confident—bold enough to walk into a bar, order a drink, even dance without a care. Lola, on the other hand, is more reserved, almost like an observer."

She nodded thoughtfully. "And when Sheena takes over, how do you feel?"

"I'm still there," the patient admitted, "but it's as if I'm watching events unfold from a distance."

"That's co-consciousness," Evelyn explained. "Even though one part is fronting, you remain aware of the others. Your brain compartmentalizes experiences, so when Sheena acts, it feels separate—even though it's still you."

The woman's eyes drifted downward. "Sometimes, though, they seem completely real. Sheena even looks like my mum in her youth, with that commanding presence, while Lola mirrors the quiet strength I remember in my grandmother. Why do they take on these forms?"

"It's not uncommon for alters to reflect figures who've shaped our lives," replied Dr. Hartley softly. "They carry qualities—sometimes admired, sometimes necessary—that you needed but couldn't fully embody on your own. They're not just imagined; they're parts of your inner world with distinct memories and roles."

A moment of silence settled between them. "So, when I lose track of what happens, it's not that I'm dreaming it up—it's that another part is stepping forward?"

"Exactly," Dr. Hartley said, offering a reassuring smile. "Understanding them is the first step toward understanding yourself."

Hannah nodded slowly, her thoughts tangled. The words settled over her, heavy yet illuminating. If Sheena and Lola were more than fragments—if they were echoes of something deeper—then what else had she buried?

A flicker of something surfaced. A feeling, distant but sharp.

A memory.

Her fingers curled against the fabric of the couch as the past pulled at her, whispering at the edges of her mind.

She was there again.

And just like that, she was no longer in the therapist's office—she was back *there.*

Chapter Twenty: Starting From the Middle - 2016

Something about airports made Hannah feel like she was in a world of endless possibilities. Each one had its own unique energy—some grand and modern, transforming the mundane act of waiting into an experience.

Changi Airport in Singapore was one of those places where thoughtful touches made the layover more of a pleasant interlude than a tiresome delay. The lush indoor gardens, the cascading waterfall, and the tranquil koi ponds offered enough distractions to keep the anxiety of travel at bay.

She was halfway to her destination, having managed to sleep through most of the first leg of her journey from the UK. Yet, her nerves still felt raw. This trip had been a spur-of-the-moment decision—one she hadn't entirely thought through. When she told Fiona, the elderly woman she had grown close to, about her imminent departure, the woman's face softened with concern.

"Why, sweetheart? What's happened? I thought you were happy here. And what about that handsome young man—Chase?"

"It's a long story, Fi. And I can't get into it now. But I've arranged for most of my things to go into storage. I thought you might like to keep some of my drawings. Or, if you don't want them, you can give them away."

"Nonsense!" Fiona scoffed, taking the offered sketches with care. "How else will I remember you and all the lovely times we've shared?" Then, her expression grew more serious. "Look, hon, I know there are things you don't want to talk about. I see it in your eyes. I recognize that pain—I've carried it, too. But promise me one thing: don't keep it all inside. It will eat you up if you do."

Hannah had simply nodded and hugged Fiona, the two women exchanging a final wave as Fiona dropped her off at the airport.

Now, halfway across the world, waiting in line at a deli before her next flight, her mind drifted. Would she ever see Fiona again? What exactly was she planning to do when she arrived in Melbourne? The uncertainty gnawed at her, making her stomach twist with unease.

She was so lost in thought that she didn't notice the person standing behind her until she bumped into him.

"Oh, my goodness, I'm so sorry! I should watch where I'm going. Blame the jet lag!" she exclaimed, turning to face him.

The man, around her age, had striking blue eyes, a shaved head, and an effortlessly Scandinavian look. His crisp white t-shirt contrasted with his tanned skin, and he exuded an air of easy confidence.

"Ah, no worries. I wasn't paying attention either," he said with a warm laugh, revealing perfectly white teeth. "Actually, I think we were on the same flight from the UK."

"Really?" Hannah asked, catching an interesting accent laced into his words.

"Yeah, you were sitting a few aisles ahead of me."

"Sorry, I must have slept through most of it," she admitted. She had taken a relaxant before takeoff, hoping to numb her nerves.

"Where are you headed?" he asked as he paid for his drink, and they walked out of the deli together, wheeling their hand luggage behind them.

"Melbourne," she said, feeling a strange comfort in saying it aloud.

"No way! Me too!" He grinned, a flicker of curiosity lighting his expression. "Maybe we'll end up as seatmates."

Hannah chuckled. "Maybe."

"So, are you visiting, or do you live there?" she asked.

"My father lives in Melbourne. I've visited a couple of times before, but this time, I might stay longer—find a job, maybe study a bit." He glanced at her, his eyes assessing. "And you?"

She hesitated. She wasn't ready to explain. In truth, she wasn't entirely sure herself.

"It's… a personal visit," she said vaguely, shifting her gaze away.

He nodded, as if sensing not to pry. "Well, it's nice to meet you. I'm Alexander." He extended his hand toward her.

"I'm—" She hesitated for a split second before offering a small smile. "*Sheena.*" She reached out, shaking his hand, the name tasting foreign yet strangely familiar on her tongue.

Chapter Twenty-One: One Step Forward, Two Steps Backwards (2016)

"**A**re you okay? You seem... distant?" Jen asked, her gaze fixed on the man sitting across from her. It had been almost four months since they had started dating, yet she still couldn't quite define what they were.

They had met online; he had liked her profile, and she had initiated a conversation. He was the first guy she had spoken to who could hold an engaging discussion without resorting to inappropriate messages or unsolicited photos of a certain part of his anatomy. That alone had set him apart.

Jen had avoided reactivating her dating profile on OkCupid for a long time. Each time she gave it another chance, she found herself disappointed by the calibre of men she met. But Brett was different. He seemed genuinely interested in knowing her.

They had bonded over their shared love for photography and camping and even discovered they were both INFJ personality types. Conversations with him flowed naturally, yet there was a reluctance on his part—an invisible wall she couldn't quite scale.

"Do you think there's someone else in the picture?" Lisa, her closest friend, had once asked. But Jen had shaken her head. "I don't think so. I just feel like he's afraid of getting hurt or something."

Now, sitting together at her place over dinner, the usual warmth between them had given way to a heavy tension. Brett wasn't as engaged as he usually was.

"Jen, I think there's something you should know," he said at last, his voice measured, his expression troubled. He met her eyes before continuing. "My ex—Hannah—she's back in Melbourne. And... it has totally caught me off guard."

"Your ex?" Jen's heart sank. "You mean the one you had a child with? The one you—" She trailed off, not wanting to finish the sentence.

It had taken Brett a while to talk about his past, about Hannah and the child they had lost and about his dad, who had been sick for a long time but was slowly recovering, though still quite unwell.

When he had finally told her, the revelation had shaken her, yet it also deepened her connection with him. She had never experienced such loss herself, but she had wondered what it must have been like for him.

She had also questioned whether he had ever truly moved on. He had said therapy helped, that keeping busy made things easier. He had admitted that he missed Hannah and that he had tried reaching out but had come to accept that she was gone. That he was ready to move forward.

But now...

"Seeing her again has made me realize I still have some unresolved emotions," Brett confessed, his voice low, his expression clouded with sadness.

"You still love her?" The question escaped Jen before she could stop it. The answer, she feared, would shatter her.

An agonizing silence stretched between them before Brett gave a slow, almost reluctant nod.

Jen was quiet for a long moment, her mind spinning, her chest tightening with unspoken emotions. When she finally spoke, her voice was steady, but there was a weight behind it. "Then you need to figure out what you want, Brett. You and Hannah share a deep history—a painful past that isn't easy to move on from. If she's back in your life, I... I don't know where that leaves me." She hesitated, struggling to contain the storm brewing inside her.

She had underestimated just how much she felt for him, and now, before she could even tell him, it was already slipping away.

She inhaled sharply before continuing, "I really like you, Brett. But I can't be with someone who's still trying to figure out whether they want to be with someone else."

Brett looked at her, his expression filled with regret and sorrow. "I'm so sorry, Jen. I never meant to put you in this position. I thought I was ready to move on... I really did. But seeing her again..." He exhaled heavily, rubbing his face with his hands. "God, I've made such a mess of things."

Jen blinked back tears, her throat tightening. "It's okay, Brett. You need to take your time and figure out what will truly make you happy. But I can't wait around for you to decide." Her voice was soft but resolute. "I like you a lot. But I must protect myself, too."

Her voice wavered slightly, and the tears spilled over before she could stop them. She wiped at them quickly, unwilling to let them take control. Brett reached out instinctively as if to comfort her but stopped himself, realizing he had no right to.

The silence between them was deafening. And in that silence, Jen knew this was the end—at least for now.

...——— ⚜ ———...

It had been over a week since Hannah had knocked at his door and left his world reeling. Seeing her again had brought back emotions he thought he had buried, unravelling him in a way he hadn't expected. Nights had become restless, filled with sleepless hours of tossing and turning, trying to make sense of what it all meant.

"Hi, Brett," Hannah had said, standing in his doorway like a ghost from his past.

"Hannah?" His voice was barely above a whisper, disbelief etched into his features. He had envisioned this moment countless times, yearning for it yet fearing what it might mean. And now, here she was—real, present, and standing before him. "What—what are you doing here?" he asked, stepping aside to let her in.

"I wasn't sure if you still lived here. You sent me your address a while ago. I—I finally read all your emails."

His breath caught. "I didn't even know if you were receiving them. I kept sending them anyway. Why—why didn't you ever respond? I was worried sick about you. I even thought about flying to the UK to find you, but I had no idea where to start. You just... vanished."

"We agreed it was for the best, Brett. We were both drowning in grief. I needed time—space to heal," Hannah said, her voice fragile.

They sat silently, the weight of unspoken words pressing down on them. At last, Brett spoke. "I've missed you. So much. I can't tell you how happy I am to see you."

Hannah gave him a tremulous smile. "It wasn't until I was on my way here that I realized how much I might be disrupting your life. I'm sorry I didn't reach out sooner. But seeing your emails, the photos... It made me realize how much I missed you. And I miss her, too."

Her voice cracked, and the tears spilled over before she could hold back. She sobbed, unrestrained, the weight of years of grief breaking through.

Without hesitation, Brett moved, pulling her into his arms. They clung to each other, the past and present colliding.

Chapter Twenty-Two:
Chrissie (April 2011)

Chrissie sat in her stroller, her tiny fingers gripping the plush rabbit Brett had bought her at the market that morning.

The scent of freshly cut grass and warm earth filled the air as they strolled through the park. The laughter of children echoed from the nearby playground, the metallic creak of swings blending with the distant chirping of birds. She kicked her legs excitedly, her chubby toes wiggling in the air as they neared the play area close to the beach.

"Want to go on the swings, bub?" Brett asked, crouching beside her. His voice was warm, familiar. She didn't understand all his words, but she knew that tone—it meant fun, laughter, something exciting about to happen.

She babbled in response, reaching her arms up to him. Brett grinned, unbuckling her carefully and lifting her onto his shoulders.

At just fourteen months old, the world seemed bigger from up there, the sky stretching endlessly above them. She squealed as he bounced her gently, her hands patting his hair.

Hannah walked beside them, her gaze flicking between the playground and the two of them. "Careful," she murmured, though her lips curved into a soft smile.

Brett spun them in a slow circle, his laughter rumbling in his chest. "Mummy says to be careful, Chrissie. What do you think? Should we be careful?"

Chrissie clapped her hands together, giggling. She didn't know what careful meant. But she knew she liked how her Daddy held her, how the breeze tickled her cheeks, and how the sun warmed her skin.

Brett gently set her down as they reached the swings, guiding her small hands to the chains. "Ready?" he asked, his grin wide.

Chrissie let out a delighted squeal as he pushed her, the world tilting and swaying in a rhythm that made her giggle uncontrollably. She looked back at him, eyes wide with excitement, the wind sweeping through her curls.

Hannah sat on the nearby bench, watching them with quiet warmth. For now, in this moment, everything was perfect.

But time was fleeting. The days were slipping away too quickly, like sand through grasping fingers.

Soon, the warmth of this afternoon, the sound of Chrissie's laughter, the innocent trust in her wide eyes—all would be memories.

No one knew what lay ahead or how a single moment could change everything. The weight of what was to come lingered just beyond reach, unseen yet inevitable.

The ocean stretched out before them, its surface glistening under the afternoon sun. As Brett lifted her from the swing's harness, she instinctively reached for Hannah, her tiny fingers grasping at her mother's shirt before nestling into her arms, her warmth pressing close.

Hannah pressed a kiss to her forehead, murmuring something soft, something safe.

Chrissie didn't have all the words yet, but she knew this: she was loved, and the world was perfect in that moment.

Chapter Twenty - Three: A Fractured Reality (2016)

It always started the same way—Hannah jolting awake in the middle of the night, gasping for air, Chrissie's name slipping from her lips like a desperate prayer. Her skin was damp with sweat, her breathing erratic, as if she had been running for miles in a nightmare she could never escape.

Brett had watched helplessly as this became a pattern, his heart aching for her. He had suggested therapy—couples therapy, something they could navigate together—but after only a few weeks, Hannah pulled away.

"I thought you were finding it helpful?" Brett asked one evening as they strolled hand in hand along a quiet path, the soft glow of streetlights casting elongated shadows around them.

"Well... yes. To an extent," she admitted hesitantly. "But I—I just don't feel mentally ready for some aspects of it."

Brett glanced at her; his brow furrowed. "Would you rather do the sessions alone?"

She shook her head, her gaze drifting toward the distant horizon.

"No. It's just that... when I was in the UK, I processed things in my own way, at my own pace." She hesitated. "Being back here with you—it feels right, but I need to keep myself occupied."

She glanced at him then, a small, uncertain smile forming. "You have your photography and your design gigs—I need something too. I've been thinking about going back to uni. Maybe enrolling in a course."

A pause, then a quiet exhale. "I actually managed to finish my bachelor's while I was there."

A flicker of something close to excitement crossed her face. "Studying and focusing on my artwork helped me back then. I want to continue doing that here."

Brett nodded, relieved to hear a plan forming in her mind. "That sounds great. Whatever you need, I'm here to support you."

She grinned suddenly. "Maybe I'll try something new—like baking – or photography, even! I could set up my own little side hustle. Imagine that!"

Brett chuckled. "Whoa, hold up there, Martha Stewart. You've got a whole list of ambitions lined up!" He pulled her close, inhaling the familiar scent of her hair, a warmth spreading through his chest. He had missed this—the light in her eyes, the way she leaned into him.

But just days after that hopeful evening, things took a turn Brett hadn't anticipated.

That Saturday morning, he had woken up to an empty bed. Strange. They usually slept in on weekends, savouring the slow starts to the day.

He got up, stretching, and then he heard her voice—a low murmur coming from the guest room. She had closed the door but sounded animated and engaged in a conversation with someone.

He hesitated, then knocked lightly before pushing the door open. "Hey, do you want some coffee?"

Silence.

Hannah—or rather, the woman who sat on the edge of the bed—looked up at him, startled. There was no phone in her hand, no sign of a conversation partner.

"Who were you talking to?" Brett asked, scanning the empty room.

She met his gaze, her expression unreadable. "*Chrissie.*"

His stomach tightened. "Chrissie?"

"I talk to her sometimes." Her voice was steady, as if this was the most natural thing in the world. "That's okay, isn't it?"

Brett stepped inside, sitting beside her. "Do you do this often?" he asked gently.

She shrugged. "It started after I got back. I feel like... she's here. Part of the reason I returned was to be closer to her."

Brett's heart ached at the weight of her words. "You can talk to me about it, you know?"

She nodded but said nothing more, the distance between them stretching like an invisible chasm.

A few days later, Brett tentatively suggested they visit Chrissie's grave—something he had done every year without fail. But the moment the words left his lips, Hannah froze.

"I don't want to do that."

Her voice was barely above a whisper, but the sheer force of emotion behind it made Brett's breath hitch.

"I'm sorry," she added quickly. "I just... I can't. I don't need to go there to feel close to her."

Before he could respond, she grabbed her keys and left the house. Hours later, she returned, her face bright with excitement as she burst through the door.

"I enrolled in a course at uni!" she announced, beaming. "It's going to be amazing! I've already met some people—they all seem great. I can't wait to get started."

Brett blinked at her sudden transformation. Just that morning, she had been on the verge of breaking apart, and now she stood before him, smiling as if nothing had happened.

"That's... great, Hannah," he said, forcing a smile though unease gnawed at him.

He wanted to ask if she was *really* okay. If she had slept at all. If the nightmares were still haunting her. But before he could get the words out, she turned to him, her eyes burning with something unrecognizable.

"Look, Brett," she said firmly. "*Sheena.* That's my name. Stop calling me Hannah."

Brett's heart pounded. His breath caught in his throat.

"What?" He barely managed to let out the word.

"You heard me," she said, her expression defiant.

He stared at her, trying to make sense of the woman standing before him. His Hannah—the woman he loved—was slipping away, replaced by someone else. And he wasn't sure how to bring her back.

...— — — ⚜ — — —...

Some weeks after enrolling in her course, she made an announcement that left Brett reeling.

"I'm moving," she said one evening, casually, as if discussing the weather. "Somewhere closer to the city."

The words hung in the air, sharp and unexpected, slicing through the quiet hum of the television. Brett turned to look at her, searching her face for something—hesitation, second thoughts—anything to indicate that this was just an idea she was toying with. But Sheena had already made up her mind.

Again. She was leaving again.

The tension between them had been simmering for weeks, but it boiled over on Halloween night. Brett had waited up for her, watching the hours slip by, each one thick with unease.

Midnight passed. Then, 1 a.m. Finally, the sound of the front door unlocking made him exhale a breath he hadn't realized he was holding.

She stepped inside, swaying slightly, her heels clicking against the floor, her laughter still echoing from the night's revelry. She was still dressed as a dark angel—black feathers lining her shoulders, smoky eyeliner framing her brown eyes, and lips-stained crimson. She looked different. Still beautiful, but different. Like someone he didn't quite recognize.

She wasn't Hannah. Not really.

Hannah had been soft-spoken and introspective, someone who loved warm tea and long conversations that stretched deep into the night. She laughed at his bad jokes, asked him questions about his design gigs, and made their world feel like a safe cocoon.

Sheena was electric. Sharp-witted. There was something untamed about her, something reckless and racy that made her feel almost untouchable. He had caught glimpses of Sheena before—back when they lived with his parents, just before everything fell apart. She questioned his parents and resented his dad quite openly. But she had been fleeting back then, a temporary spark in the dark. Now, she was fully here.

"You won't believe who I bumped into at the party!" she said, shrugging off her coat as she walked past him.

"Alex! The guy from the airport in Singapore! Turns out he's at my uni. What are the odds of that?" She chuckled to herself, her tone light, carefree. She didn't even acknowledge that he had been waiting up.

Brett felt something twist inside him.

"You didn't answer my calls," he said, his voice controlled but edged with frustration. "I was worried about you, Hann—Sheena." He caught himself just in time.

She turned to face him, her expression instantly darkening.

"I'm not a child, Brett," she snapped. "I told you I'd be out late. You didn't have to wait up for me."

Her words stung. It wasn't just what she said but how she said it—like he was nothing more than an afterthought.

"Is that why you ignored my calls?" he shot back, his jaw tightening. "Not even a text to let me know that you're okay?"

She let out a slow, tired sigh as if he was exhausting her. "I'm not in the mood for this. I've had a long day and just want to shower and sleep."

And just like that, she walked past him, disappearing down the hallway without another word.

Brett stood there for a long time, staring after her, feeling something between them shifting—something slipping away.

Chapter Twenty-Four: She's Gone

Sheena was on her way home from work when her phone rang. It was her dad. She had missed his calls earlier and had meant to return them once she got home.

The day had been a whirlwind—morning classes at uni, hours spent poring over research as a part-time assistant in the Art and Design Faculty, and an evening promise to grab drinks with a few friends.

For most Melburnians, 2022 was the year of catching up from the longest stretch of lockdowns and social distancing, which was still marked by a sense of unease and tentative mask-wearing.

Now, she was heading home for a quick shower and dinner before rushing back out. The busyness had been deliberate. She had wanted to drown in it, especially after leaving Brett to live alone. And now, she was completely submerged.

She had hoped to call her dad when she was ready—when she had the emotional energy to face the conversation.

Their last exchange had been short and perfunctory, touching on her coursework and whether she had settled in properly. He had mentioned Italy and Martha, and she had somewhat absently promised to visit again soon.

Now, with the phone ringing in her hand, she wondered what had changed. What he needed to say that couldn't wait.

She answered. "Oh, hi, Daddy. I'm sorry I missed your calls earlier. It's been a really busy day. How are you and Martha doing?"

"Hannah."

She flinched. The name was like a ghost—one she had buried deep. But she said nothing.

"Hannah, are you home? Is someone with you?" His voice was thick, tinged with something unsettling.

She stopped walking. A chill crept up her spine. "No, but I'm almost there. Just a couple of minutes away. Why? What's wrong?" A familiar sense of dread coiled around her ribs, squeezing tight.

Her father hesitated. "Maybe you should get home first."

"No, Dad. Just tell me now. What happened?"

A heavy sigh, as though he were bracing himself. "It's your mum, Hannah. She's... she's gone. She died in her sleep."

The rest of his words blurred into an incoherent hum. Sheena stopped dead in her tracks, staring blankly at the world around her—the traffic humming by, a couple walking their dog, a man approaching with a pizza box, chatting on his phone. Life was moving on, unaware that hers had just shattered - again.

She didn't remember how she got home. Didn't remember what she said to her father after that. She only remembered the weightlessness of it all, the slow unravelling of everything inside her.

Memories flooded in, a violent rush breaking through the dam she had carefully built. Her world was cracking, piece by piece.

...———⚜———...

Months had passed since Sheena had moved into her studio apartment closer to uni. And Brett—Brett had thought about reaching out to her. But he had stopped himself every time. It wouldn't be fair, not to her, not to himself.

Just because Hannah—no, Sheena—had left didn't mean he had stopped missing her. It didn't mean he had stopped hoping. He worried about her. Still called sometimes, just to check in. But she had built a different life now; one that didn't seem to have space for him.

So, he threw himself into work—freelance design gigs, anything to keep his mind occupied. Then, his father's health had taken yet another turn for the worse. Another stroke. More hospital visits. More late nights balancing responsibilities, trying to be the pillar his mother needed.

It was just before the Easter holidays when he finally heard from her. A simple text: *I lost my mum.*

He didn't hesitate. He grabbed his keys and drove straight to her.

When she opened the door, he barely recognized her. Her eyes were hollowed out, red-rimmed from too many nights of crying. Her hair was tangled, her body slack with exhaustion. She looked fragile in a way that scared him.

He stayed with her that weekend, holding her through the nights, making sure she ate, coaxing her into moments of sleep, though it never lasted long. She would jolt awake, breathless, haunted by dreams she wouldn't talk about.

Something had shifted in her. The sharp-edged, guarded Sheena was gone—or at least, buried beneath the weight of her grief. There was a stillness about her now, a quiet detachment. And then there was Chrissie.

She talked about her again. More than before. As if she were real. As if she were in the room with them. At first, Brett didn't say anything. He didn't want to take that from her if she needed it to cope. But he saw it happening. Slowly, subtly.

Sheena was fading. And in her place, someone else was emerging - Lola.

Brett had always known Sheena was different, but he hadn't fully understood the extent of it until now. Her shifts—the way she morphed from sharp-witted and independent to quiet and withdrawn—were no longer just changes in mood. It was as if different pieces of her were fighting for control.

As time passed, he started noticing how she'd refer to herself in different ways. Some days, she'd talk about things Sheena had done as if she were a separate person. Other times, she'd slip into Lola's habits—softer, more hesitant, more unsure of herself.

And then there were the moments she was Hannah again—the most challenging moments of all. The ones where she looked at him with all the pain and weight of their past. The ones where she remembered Chrissie as their little girl, whom they had lost. And the ones where she didn't.

It was a gradual realization, one that came in pieces. The more he saw it, the harder it became to ignore. Sheena wasn't just one person. And neither was Lola. And neither was Hannah.

She was all of them. And somehow, she was none of them.

Chapter Twenty-Five: A Reunion

The fourteen-hour flight to Melbourne had not been as gruelling as Tomiwa Macaulay had expected. There had been turbulence during the final stretch, jolting the plane as though it were a paper boat on stormy waters.

Across the aisle, a young woman gripped the armrests so tightly her knuckles whitened, her eyes wide with barely restrained panic. He, however, sat calm and composed, his fingers loosely clasped in his lap. Years of travel as a diplomat had inured him to the stomach-lurching dips and sudden jolts of air travel. These days, turbulence barely registered.

Still, it was strange to think how different his life had become since retiring. The frenetic pace of international diplomacy, with its endless flights and whirlwind schedules, had given way to a peaceful existence in Italy. Life with Martha was quiet, rooted, and richly satisfying, a far cry from the constant packing and unpacking that once defined his world. He could hardly believe he'd lived that way for decades.

Now, standing at the baggage carousel, he found himself almost reluctant to confront what awaited him on the other side of those sliding airport doors.

As he reached into his pocket to power up his phone, he felt a light tap on his shoulder. It was the young woman from the flight.

"Will you be okay finding your way?" she asked, her voice bright but tinged with concern. "My brother's picking me up. We could drop you off if you need a ride. You practically saved me from passing out up there." She flashed him a grateful smile, her eyes crinkling at the corners.

He chuckled softly. "Ah, it was nothing. I enjoyed our conversation—it made the time fly by."

She'd been terrified during the turbulence, her anxiety palpable, so he'd distracted her with stories. He'd asked about her holiday in Santorini, listening as she described the sun-drenched beaches and glittering waters. He'd shared a little about his trip, hinting at the estranged daughter he hoped to reconnect with in Melbourne. She reminded him of Hannah—young, earnest, and full of life.

"Thank you for the offer, but my daughter and her boyfriend are picking me up," he said.

"Ah, got it. Well, good luck with everything. I hope you enjoy Melbourne—and don't forget to check out the Queen Vic Market! Maybe I'll see you there!" she said with a grin before wheeling her suitcase away and disappearing into the crowd.

The buzz of his phone broke through his thoughts. It was a message from Hannah, short and to the point: *We're parking now. Meet you in Arrivals soon.* He could sense a quiver of nervousness in the words—or perhaps it was his own anxiety mirrored back at him. After all, it had been six years. Six long years since he'd last seen her.

The memory was still vivid: Hannah was standing in the courtyard of a small villa in Tuscany with a tentative smile on her lips as she wished him and Martha well. She'd stayed just long enough to offer her congratulations, pressing a kiss to his cheek before leaving.

Her promises to visit had gone unfulfilled. Calls and messages dwindled, reduced to obligatory holiday greetings. And then, after her mother—his ex-wife—passed away, she had gone silent altogether. He had reached out repeatedly, desperate for even a flicker of response. Nothing.

Until Brett, her boyfriend, had contacted him weeks before.

"She needs you," Brett had said. "She won't say it, but she does."

Martha had offered to join him on this trip, but he'd refused. This was something he had to do alone. There were bridges to mend, questions to answer, and years of regret to face.

And now, there was no turning back.

"Dad?"

The voice startled him. It was familiar yet strange, tinged with the softness of memory and the sharpness of time. He turned, and there she was.

Hannah stood a few paces away, her face framed by strands of dark, wavy curls that fell loosely over her shoulders. She was thinner than he remembered, her features more angular, but she was unmistakably his daughter. Her eyes, a mirror of his own, held a mixture of apprehension and hope.

"Hello, Hannah," he said, his voice catching.

He stepped forward, pulling her into a tight embrace. She hesitated for the briefest moment before melting into his arms.

"My darling girl," he murmured, his voice trembling as tears filled his eyes. They slipped silently down his cheeks, soaking into her hair. For the first time in years, he allowed himself to feel the weight of his failures—and the fragile, flickering possibility of redemption.

Chapter Twenty - Six: Down Memory Lane

It had been a restless night for everyone, but the unease went far beyond jet lag for Tom. The time difference and the unfamiliar bed were trivial compared to the lingering pain of the previous evening.

Six years ago, when Hannah had flown in briefly from Australia to attend Tom's wedding to his second wife, he had gently tried to talk about the loss of Chrissie, his granddaughter. Yet, overwhelmed by her grief, Hannah had steered clear of the conversation, and Tom, not wanting to cause her further hurt, had reluctantly let the subject drop.

Now, as he lay awake, every word she'd spoken and every flicker of sorrow in her eyes replayed in his mind, deepening the weight of her pain—and his own sense of responsibility for it.

A soft knock broke the stillness of the morning.

"Dad?" Hannah's voice came from the other side of the door.

He shuffled to the door and opened it to find her standing there, her eyes searching his face. "Brett's making omelettes. You should eat something. You didn't have that much at dinner last night," she said, her voice tentative.

Her dad offered her a tired smile. "I wasn't very hungry. But neither were you," he countered, studying her face as though searching for clues he had missed before.

She shrugged, looking down. "I was nervous. I haven't seen you in so long... And I didn't even know Brett had been in contact with you. I didn't know he had your number after you moved to Italy." Her voice wavered, and she hesitated before continuing.

"He always wanted to know more about you and Mum, to keep that connection alive. But I... I didn't. I thought I could start over here. A clean slate.

I didn't think he'd go behind my back to reach out to you, but now... I know it was unfair of me to expect him to carry that burden alone."

Tom sighed, stepping aside to let her in. "Hannah, I'm glad he reached out. Truly. He did the right thing. I only wish it had been sooner. But I understand why he waited. He was trying to respect your wishes."

He paused, his voice softening. "I just feel so sad that you thought you couldn't reach out to me and went through everything alone. I failed you, Hannah. And for that, I'm so, so sorry."

Hannah's composure cracked, "I'm sorry, too. I just... I didn't want to be a burden. I've always felt like I was this huge weight you and Mum had to carry."

Tom reached for her hands. "You were never a burden, Hannah. Never." His voice was thick with emotion, his grip gentle but firm.

He let out a slow breath, shaking his head. "I got it wrong—terribly wrong. I thought I was doing the right thing by working hard and providing for you and your mum." He paused, his gaze searching hers. "But I wasn't there, not in the way you needed me to be."

Hannah swallowed, the weight of his words settling deep in her chest.

"And your mum..." Tom hesitated, his expression clouded with something unreadable. "She wasn't distant because of you. She was scared, operating from a place of fear and hurt. She closed herself off to protect herself."

Hannah frowned, her feelings of sadness and despair momentarily forgotten. "Protect herself? From what?"

Tom hesitated, the weight of old secrets heavy on his tongue.

"She spoke to me some weeks before she... passed," he said finally, his voice thick with emotion.

Hannah's breath caught in her throat.

"It wasn't a good conversation," Tom admitted, rubbing a hand over his face. "She was upset that you had attended my wedding but hadn't gone over to see her before leaving for Melbourne." He said, his gaze distant.

"We were still blaming each other for what happened between us—for the distance between us and you." His voice grew quieter. "She never forgave me for leaving, for building a new life."

Tom's eyes met Hannah's then, raw with regret.

"And I... I couldn't forgive myself for failing you both."

He paused, running a hand through his greying hair. "But, Hannah, you need to know—your mum carried her own scars. She parented from a place of pain, of what she knew growing up."

"She never talked much about her side of the family," Hannah admitted. "I met Gran before she died, but she didn't seem keen on me. It always felt like she resented me for taking Mum away."

She recalled the few times they had visited Ireland. She was still relatively young at the time. They had always visited briefly and stayed in a hotel instead of at her granny's place.

She remembered her gran once saying something about her place not being fancy enough for them. Her granny had shown her many photos of aunts, uncles, and cousins, none of whom she ever met.

Tom nodded, his expression darkening. "Your mum's childhood was... difficult. Her family was devoutly Catholic, strict to the core, and full of expectations she refused to conform to. But that wasn't the worst of it. It wasn't why she left Ireland."

Hannah's heart quickened. "Then why?"

He took a deep breath as though steeling himself. "Your mum had an older sister, Moira. She was everything your grandparents wanted—a model daughter. Churchgoing, obedient, and engaged to an upstanding man they adored. One day, when it was just your mum at home, Moira's fiancé came by. He said he'd wait for Moira to get back from work. But instead..." His voice broke, and he looked away.

"He assaulted your mum, Hannah. And when she told her family, they didn't believe her. They accused her of being jealous and of trying to ruin Moira's life. They shamed her—and ostracized her. She left Ireland not long after."

The room was silent except for the quiet hitch of Hannah's breath. She stared at her father, her mind racing to reconcile this revelation with the fragments of her mother she had known.

"Your mum never wanted to burden you with this," He continued, his voice low and heavy with regret. "But it shaped her. It hardened her in ways she didn't know how to soften. She carried that pain into her life, into her relationships. And Hannah, she loved you. In her way, she loved you deeply. But she didn't know how to show it."

Emotion swelled in Hannah's chest, tightening her throat and stealing her words. She pressed a hand to her face, drawing in a shaky breath. When she finally spoke, her voice was barely above a whisper.

"I wish she had told me. Maybe... maybe we could have understood each other better."

Tom reached out, resting a hand on her shoulder. "It's not too late to understand, Hannah. We can piece this together—heal, even if it's slow. We owe that to her. And to ourselves."

For the first time, Hannah didn't pull away.

"I'd like to know more about you and Mum," she said, her voice soft but edged with curiosity.

"How did you meet? What was life like back then for the two of you? I remember things being a bit strained between Mum and your side of the family. I never quite understood why. And we didn't stay long enough in Nigeria for me to get to know them well."

Tom smiled wistfully, a mix of nostalgia and remorse flickering across his face. "Ah, there's so much to tell, so many gaps to fill. Your mum and I had quite the story. We met in London during my postgraduate studies in Economics. I was full of ambition and naivety back then. She was different from anyone I'd ever met—bold, quick-witted, and unapologetically herself." He chuckled.

"She challenged me in ways I didn't know I needed. Life was hectic back then, but we carved out something of our own amidst all the chaos."

He paused, his voice thickening with emotion. "I brought some mementos with me. Things from the past that I thought you might want to see. Photos, a couple of your dolls, and some of your artwork from when we lived in France. I found them at your mum's place while clearing it out."

Tom hesitated before adding, "She kept so many of your things, Hannah. Even after you left, I think it was her way of holding onto you. She missed you more than she ever let on. You and Christina."

Hannah's expression softened, her gaze dropping to the floor as she processed his words. After a moment, she nodded, blinking away the emotions welling in her eyes. "I'd like to see those things," she said, smiling faintly. Then, as if sensing the need to shift the conversation, she took a breath and smiled faintly. "But first, come have breakfast. Afterwards, we can take a walk, and I'll show you a bit of the neighbourhood."

Tom smiled back, grateful for her effort to lighten the mood. "That sounds like a good plan. I could use some food. Did Brett make an Australian omelette?"

Hannah stopped and turned to him with a mock-serious expression. "Dad! You're ridiculous. It's just an omelette. I don't think it's an *Aussie* one, but I hope that doesn't make it less special or delicious for you!"

Tom chuckled, the warmth in her teasing lifting a weight he hadn't realized he was carrying. Hearing her laugh for the first time since he'd arrived filled him with a quiet joy.

"I'm sure it'll be perfect," he said, following her to the door.

As they walked toward the kitchen, Tom couldn't help but feel a glimmer of hope. It wasn't just the lighthearted banter but the sense of something rebuilding between them. Piece by piece, they were beginning to bridge the distance that had once seemed insurmountable.

Chapter Twenty-Seven: Some More Revelations

The Yarra River gleamed under the soft morning light, its surface rippling gently with the occasional breeze. The air was crisp but promised a warmer afternoon, as it often did in Melbourne's unpredictable spring.

Along the riverbank in Hawthorn, the trail meandered like a ribbon through towering eucalypts and graceful weeping willows. The trees leaned over the water, their reflections dancing in the river's flow, while bursts of wattle blooms added cheerful splashes of yellow to the scene.

Hannah and her dad walked at a leisurely pace, their footsteps crunching against the gravel path.

The scent of damp earth mingled with the faint, bracing tang of eucalyptus, grounding them in the heart of nature despite the suburban hum in the distance. A gentle whoosh and rhythmic splash drew their attention to a group of rowers slicing through the water with practised precision.

"Isn't that something?" Tom said, pausing to watch the crew glide in perfect unison, their brightly colored jerseys vivid against the muted tones of the riverbank. Their oars dipped and rose in flawless synchrony, each movement a testament to discipline and muscle memory. The boat skimmed effortlessly across the water, leaving only a whisper of ripples in its wake.

"They practice every weekend," Hannah explained, gesturing toward the rowing club just visible further down the river. "You see them in the early mornings and sometimes at sunset. Brett says it's meditative to watch them. I just think it's impressive how they manage to stay so in sync."

They continued along the trail, passing joggers with earbuds in, their determined expressions softened by a friendly nod as they passed. A couple walked hand-in-hand, a leashed Labrador trotting beside them, its tail wagging eagerly. Near a wooden bench, a young family had stopped to feed the ducks, the children laughing as the birds bobbed and quacked expectantly.

"Do you remember when we fed ducks back in France?" Tom asked, his voice tinged with nostalgia.

Hannah's eyes softened as she recalled those afternoons. "I do," she said, smiling faintly. "I remember sitting by the quiet pond in the Jardin du Luxembourg, scattering a handful of grains and watching how the ducks would waddle up as if they knew a treat was coming. They'd huddle close, almost competing for every little morsel. But I think these ones might be even greedier!"

The sound of bicycles whirring by mingled with the occasional chirp of magpies and the low chatter of a group of friends stretching before a run.

Hannah guided her father toward a small lookout point where the trail widened. From there, the Yarra curved gracefully, framed by trees that formed a natural arch over the water.

"This is my favourite spot," she said quietly, leaning against the wooden railing. "I once spotted a Platypus around here."

Tom's eyes lit up. "A platypus? Really? I've never seen one in the wild."

"They're shy, but they're here," she replied, scanning the water's surface.

A rower's call and the clatter of oars interrupted the momentary quiet.

"It's beautiful, Hannah. I can see why you love it here. I think your mum would have loved it, too," her dad said, his voice soft, the weight of memory settling into his tone.

Hannah glanced at the trail ahead, sunlight filtering through the trees and dappled across the path. The faint rustle of leaves swayed in rhythm with the breeze, and she imagined her mum running here, her ponytail bouncing with every stride, her face alight with purpose.

"I think she would have loved running here," Hannah said, her voice quiet but steady. "She always loved finding new trails. It would've been her kind of place."

"That, she would've loved," her dad agreed, nodding slowly. "You know, she tried to get me into running back in the day. I gave it a shot, but I couldn't keep up! She had so much energy. Meanwhile, I felt like an old man trying to chase her down." A wry smile spread across his face, though his eyes carried a wistful shadow.

Hannah hesitated before speaking, her question hanging in the air like a fragile thread. "Did you still love her even after... everything?"

Her father exhaled, a deep, steady breath that carried years of heartache and acceptance. "I did. But as you know, love isn't enough to make things work." A wistful look crossed his face.

"Your mum and I made many sacrifices to be together. I gave up the life I'd envisioned and moved back to Nigeria after my studies in the UK. She faced resistance from both sides of the family—mine wanted a traditional Nigerian wife, and hers wanted her to settle down with some Irish lad they thought could tame her."

He chuckled dryly. "Taming your mum? That was never going to happen! But she handled it all with such grace at first. She was adventurous and fearless. She embraced Nigeria—the culture, the warmth, the vibrancy of it all."

His expression grew somber. "But over time, things changed. She started to feel restless and homesick." His voice softened as he recounted the challenges in their marriage.

"She missed her family, her friends, the familiar comforts of home," he said quietly. "She turned to drinking more than she should have. She made an effort to stop when she was pregnant with you, and for a little while afterwards, running seemed to help steady her."

He exhaled, his gaze distant. "But the loneliness crept back, especially when I started traveling more for work. She felt isolated. I tried to be there when I could, but it wasn't enough."

A heavy pause settled between them. His voice was almost a whisper when he continued.

"And after a while... well, I knew. Even before she admitted it, I knew she had started seeing someone else."

Chapter Twenty-Eight:
Secrets and Betrayals

Hannah stopped in her tracks, her breath catching. "Wait. What? Mum... Mum was with someone else?" Her voice faltered, the words unfamiliar on her tongue.

Her father's expression softened with understanding.

"Before your mum and I got together, she'd been seeing someone—a bit older than her." He paused, choosing his words carefully. "They met in London while she was settling in."

His gaze drifted, lost in old memories.

"He was... a rebel, a charmer, a Lothario—the kind of man who could captivate a room." Tom said, shaking his head slightly. "It took time for her to let him go completely, but I was patient. I knew how I felt about her."

He hesitated, a distant look on his face.

"When we moved to France, though, he resurfaced," he admitted. "She sought him out, I think. It didn't last long, but..." His voice grew quieter. "It was enough to break something between us. A betrayal we couldn't fully recover from."

"I'm sorry, Dad. That must've been awful." A pang of guilt tightened her chest, the weight of her mother's choices mingling with her own regrets.

She told her dad about Alex—how effortlessly he had slipped back into her life, weaving himself into the spaces she thought were firmly filled by Brett.

After Chrissie's death and the accident, she had fled back to the UK, determined to piece herself together. But the ghosts of her past had clung to her like shadows.

Losing Coco, her beloved companion who had been her constant source of comfort, and the inevitable end of her relationship with Chase left her feeling hollow and untethered. Loneliness became a familiar ache. Even the short-lived reconciliation with her mum had not quite worked out as she had hoped.

When she finally mustered the courage to open Brett's emails, she realized she couldn't run forever. She had to go back to Australia. Being together once again had been more gut-wrenching than she'd anticipated. They'd agreed to remain in each other's lives as friends—a bittersweet compromise.

Sheena had taken the reins of her fractured self, holding on tightly for over four years, carving out a new identity.

She enrolled in university, diving headfirst into a Philosophy degree. Uni life became her sanctuary, a place to redefine who she was—or at least who she wanted to be. And it was there, in the bustling uni life, that she'd met Alex - again.

"I told Brett a little more about Sheena a while back," she admitted, her voice quivering as the confession spilled from her lips.

"He knows she was... that I was with other people. And I know he tried to move on, too, but it didn't work out for him. Still..." Her voice faltered as she wrung her hands. "He doesn't know that Alex has been in touch." "Nothing's happened, but I know he's a part of my past I should leave firmly behind."

Her dad's brow furrowed with concern. "Alex - he is married, isn't he? It sounds like he needs to figure out his own life first. But keeping this from Brett... that's not a good idea."

He was right. Brett had always been patient with Hannah—with all parts of her. When they had rekindled their relationship a year and a half ago, just shortly after her mum had died, they'd agreed to take things slow.

They lived separately, cautiously testing whether they could make it work this time. But even with Brett's understanding nature, Lola had taken the reins again, with Sheena surfacing during moments of strain.

She panicked when Brett had proposed, asking her to marry him and finally tie the elusive knot. The proposal had sent cracks rippling through her carefully constructed world - A world where Chrissie was still alive, and Brett wasn't tied to the darkest chapters of her life.

Then came the suspicion of pregnancy and, with it, a flood of buried memories she could no longer hide from.

Lola and Sheena had reacted differently, each struggling to confront the truth in their own way. And Hannah, caught between the fractured pieces of herself, was forced to reckon with her past—a past she had spent years suppressing.

"Secrets can be corrosive," her dad said softly, breaking her spiralling thoughts.

"I know," she whispered, her throat tightening as the words caught in her chest, thinking about Brett and Alex.

"In Alex's defense, I wasn't exactly honest with him back at uni. I wasn't... me. I was someone else. Non-committal, secretive, flighty," she admitted, her voice soft, almost apologetic.

"I was Sheena. In some ways, the very things that drew me to him were the things that ultimately pulled us apart. And I'd gotten a glimpse of that world - Alex's world. The glamorous lifestyle of events, endless networking, and superficial friendships. It reminded me too much of the life you and Mum had, the life I got dragged into without ever really choosing it."

Sheena had been the dominant force when she was with Alex - fearless, untethered, and reckless, a persona she wore like armour. With him, she had leaned into that side of herself, letting Sheena take over because it felt easier than being vulnerable, easier than being Hannah. Brett, however, brought out something entirely different. With Brett, she felt closer to Hannah -grounded and reflective.

Alex had noticed the shift in her recently. "You've changed," he had said casually, almost in passing. He chalked it up to maturity, remarking how her wild edges seemed to have softened with time, as though she had simply mellowed out with age.

But he didn't know the truth. Sheena hadn't changed; she had just begun to retreat. Slowly, steadily, she was slipping further into the shadows every time Brett was near.

Sheena was still there, lingering just beneath the surface, restless and waiting. But Hannah and Lola stepped forward when Brett was around. She was quieter, softer, and more vulnerable. And that was the problem. Because Alex had fallen for Sheena, not Hannah. And deep down, she wasn't sure who she wanted to be anymore.

Her dad nodded without saying much and studied her momentarily, his gaze thoughtful, searching. "I don't know much about dissociation, but this Sheena... she sounds a lot like your mum. Am I right?"

Hannah nodded, the lump in her throat growing. It had been a few months since she'd resurfaced, with Lola and Sheena retreating into the background.

The dissociative episodes had worsened when she turned to drinking—an unhealthy coping mechanism she had adopted when she learnt about her mum's death.

Dissociative Identity Disorder, her therapist had once explained, often develops as a response to intense trauma, allowing someone to compartmentalize their experiences into distinct identities.

For Hannah, Sheena and Lola weren't just fragments of her—they were survival mechanisms, each shaped by a different need and pain.

Therapy had helped her understand this, but life had gotten in the way. For a while, Sheena and Lola had managed to coexist, their influence ebbing and flowing with the demands of her chaotic life.

"Sheena was my way of understanding Mum," Hannah admitted, her voice trembling. "Of feeling close to her. She was the part of me that wanted to live like her—fearless, untethered. Sheena could leave Brett and never look back, just like Mum could move on from us without a second thought. She was everything I wasn't brave enough to be."

Her dad placed a gentle hand on her shoulder, his voice steady. "Hannah, you're stronger than you realize. Way stronger and more courageous than your mum. You're here, facing your past, trying to understand it all. That takes courage. More than running ever did."

"Hannah," he began, his voice strained, "Even when I found out about your mum's brief affair, I still wanted to give things a chance. But I knew we had reached the end when she told me about her very careless decision. After Antoine."

He paused, his words catching in his throat. "That you had gotten pregnant... and she went ahead and—" He broke off, his voice faltering as he dropped his gaze to the ground, unable to finish the sentence.

The weight of his unfinished words hung between them like a heavy fog, pressing down on them both. The silence that followed wasn't just quiet—it was deafening, filled with the echoes of things left unsaid.

Though he couldn't bring himself to say it, the memories of that horrible day came rushing back to Hannah, vivid and unrelenting.

Hannah could still see it all in her mind's eye—the faint fluorescent glow of the clinic, harsh and sterile, casting everything in a cold light.

The biting, almost synthetic odour of disinfectant pervaded the air, merging with the soft murmur of voices and gentle footsteps beyond the closed door.

She had felt numb, utterly detached, as though her body were moving through the motions without her. But beneath that numbness was an unbearable sting of despair that she had buried so deeply it had threatened to suffocate her.

She remembered waking up groggy and disoriented, her limbs heavy and her throat dry. And there, sitting beside her, was her mother. Her face was unreadable, coldly composed, as if she were simply ticking off an item on a to-do list.

It wasn't comforting; it wasn't warm. Her mother's words, delivered with a tone of detached justification, were etched into her memory: "This was for the best, Hannah. You'll thank me one day." But she hadn't thanked her.

She hadn't felt relief, only a hollow ache that never entirely went away. They had agreed at the time—her mother had convinced her that termination was the right thing to do. The practical thing to do.

And for a while, she had let herself believe it, pushing down the doubts and grief that threatened to consume her.

What broke her wasn't the decision itself but the aftermath—the pretense, the quiet, suffocating denial that it had ever happened.

Her mother's insistence on burying it in secrecy, keeping it from her father, pretending it was just another forgotten detail in their lives. That silence, that refusal to acknowledge the pain, had left scars far deeper than the decision ever could.

Now, standing there with her father, the weight of the truth between them, Hannah felt those scars ache anew. She wanted to explain, to find the words to make him understand the impossible choices she had faced, but her voice remained trapped, tangled in a web of guilt and grief.

Her dad continued, his voice slightly unsteady.

"She said it out of spite," he admitted, his gaze fixed on a point beyond the garden. "To make me feel guilty about not being around when Antoine did what he did to you." He exhaled sharply, his hands clenching into fists.

"But it was... it is still quite hard for me to forgive her for what she made you go through." His voice wavered, thick with emotion. "You were a child! And keeping it from me—your own father." His voice cracked under the weight of the words, raw and unfiltered.

He shook his head, his expression clouded with regret.

"I don't know what she was thinking, to be honest." His tone softened, but the pain remained. "She tried justifying it by saying it would have stigmatized you... that she was protecting the two of us."

Tom let out a slow breath, his shoulders heavy.

"You from being judged," he continued, his voice quieter now. "And me... because my career was just starting to take off."

His words trailed into the morning air, dissolving into the stillness. He stared into the distance, lost in a sea of memories, his face etched with the weight of things left unsaid.

Chapter Twenty- Nine:
Forgiving Abi

Hannah sat in silence; her thoughts tangled in a storm she had never been able to quiet. The pain of that time lingered like a shadow, always just out of reach but never truly gone.

The termination had etched itself into her soul, a wound that refused to heal, haunting her in fragile moments of sleep and cutting through her thoughts when she was awake.

She had learned to carry the burden in silence, burying it deep, but its weight pressed on her still, a constant reminder of what couldn't be undone.

It had driven an unyielding wedge between her and her mother—a chasm that no amount of time or effort had managed to close. What hurt most was knowing she had tried. When she returned to the UK, she had hoped to mend the fractures, to rebuild what they'd lost. But her mother had never acknowledged the pain, had never admitted her part in the unravelling of their bond. And Hannah, afraid to shatter the fragile peace, had avoided the deeper truths. Instead, they spent their rare moments together skating the surface, filling the air with pleasantries and trivialities, while the silence beneath spoke of everything left unsaid.

"It's okay, Dad," she said softly, placing a comforting hand on his shoulder. "I am... in a better place with those memories now - I think." She offered him a faint smile, though the sadness in her eyes betrayed her attempt at reassurance.

He nodded, but his expression remained clouded, the weight of the past pressing heavily on his features. "Your mum was very remorseful, though," he said, his voice tinged with a mix of regret and lingering anger. "Especially toward the end."

Hannah's lips tightened into a thin line. "She certainly had a way of showing it," she replied, her tone sharper than she intended, bitterness lacing her words.

She breathed out slowly, trying to steady herself, but the memories surged forward like an unstoppable tide. "Why was it so easy for her to let me go? After you two split, it was like she didn't even care enough to fight for me. She made hardly any effort to share custody."

Her voice wavered, but she pressed forward. 'And later—when I was older—it was as if none of it had ever happened. She rewrote history, acting like she'd never left me to figure things out alone. I know she wanted to rebuild a relationship with me, but... it was just too hard. It was like the distance between us had grown so wide that neither of us could bridge it anymore."

The memories stung like a reopened wound, raw and unhealed. She thought back to the last time she saw her mum, a strained lunch where her mother had been too consumed by her own heartbreak even to notice Hannah's pain.

Abi had been distracted, preoccupied with the bitterness of her husband moving on with another woman.

She rarely dwelled on Chrissie, hardly ever asking how her daughter was coping with the loss that had changed her life forever. On the few occasions, the topic came up, she glossed over it.

Chrissie had been her granddaughter, yet she behaved as if her absence was something best left unspoken.

Her father sighed deeply, his shoulders sagging under the weight of the truth.

"Deep down, she knew she'd let you down. What happened to you and Chrissie hit her very hard, though she never really spoke about it. She took to drinking even more." he said quietly. "And she spent the rest of her life paying for it... just in all the wrong ways."

Hannah looked at him, her expression softening as she caught the flicker of pain in his eyes.

"After the separation, your mum turned to drinking," he admitted, his voice quiet but heavy. "She said it helped her cope, but it only worsened things."

He sighed, running a hand through his greying beard.

"She was in and out of rehab for years, Hannah. It was a constant battle—one she could never fully win." His gaze dropped to the ground, as if weighed down by the memories.

"She convinced herself that keeping her distance was somehow protecting you," he continued, his voice thick with emotion. "That it was better for you not to see her like that. She thought she was sparing you, but... it created more damage."

He paused, swallowing hard before he went on.

"At the end of it all, I think it was the drinking that took her," he murmured. "Her dreams, her potential... all of it."

For a moment, he seemed lost in thought, before adding, "For a while after we split, she actually did well. She set up her own event planning business—had a real knack for it." He let out a slow, heavy breath.

"But it all got a bit too much for her." His voice was barely above a whisper now, as though saying it out loud made it all the more real.

Hannah felt a lump rise in her throat as she watched her father's eyes glisten with unshed tears. He looked smaller somehow, his pain etched deeply into his features, as if the weight of everything they had both endured had finally caught up with him.

Hannah looked away, her thoughts drifting back to her childhood. She remembered the void her mother's absence left and how her paternal grandmother—*Grandma Nigeria*, as she lovingly called her—had stepped in to fill it.

Her grandmother's presence had been a beacon of light in those dark times. She had been her anchor, holding the family together when everything else seemed to fall apart. Her grandma had always called her by her Nigerian name—Temilola—*Lola*.

Hannah smiled faintly as she recalled the warm, comforting smell of her grandmother's cooking, the rhythmic cadence of her voice as she told stories of Nigeria and the trips they had taken together to visit their extended family.

Those visits had been a balm to her young, aching heart. The vibrant colours of the Nigerian markets, the infectious laughter of cousins she had just met, and the deliciously spicy food had offered her a world so far removed from the pain back in France.

"Grandma always said mum loved me, even if I couldn't see it," Hannah murmured, her voice thick with emotion.

"She tried so hard to make me believe it. But it's hard to reconcile her absence with love. And for a long time, I blamed you, too. I thought maybe somehow you had been the one to stop her from going ahead with shared custody."

Hannah paused for a bit before saying with a hint of anger, "I also resented you for making us move around so much. It felt like we could never settle down - like we were always uprooted because of your job as a diplomat. Always another country, another language, another school. It was hard to make friends when I knew I'd have to leave them behind."

Her father's eyes softened as he looked at her. "I'm sorry, Hannah. I know those years weren't easy, Hannah. My work as a diplomat meant a lot of moving and instability, and I can see how that disrupted your sense of home. But I hoped, through it all, that you knew I was doing my best to provide for us and give you opportunities to see the world. It wasn't perfect, and I wish I could have given you more consistency." He said.

"Your grandma was right, Hannah. Your mum did love you. She just..., well, *we* didn't know how to show it in the way that we ought to have. Not in the ways you needed. I remember once, she spent hours knitting you a scarf for winter, but she never gave it to you because she was afraid it wasn't good enough." He said, looking sad.

"She always second-guessed herself when it came to you. She knew she let you down," her father said gently. "Like when she promised to come to your school play and didn't attend. But I believe she was trying, in her own flawed way, to juggle everything and be there for you as best as she could."

"Maybe," Hannah murmured, her voice barely audible. "But sometimes love isn't enough. Actions matter, too." She looked away, her gaze unfocused as memories surfaced, sharp and bittersweet.

For so long after her mum's death, she had felt tangled in a web of emotions—anger, confusion, guilt. So many words had gone unsaid after she returned to Australia, so many chances lost.

When her dad called to tell her that her mum had died in her sleep, the words felt unreal—like the punchline to a cruel joke she wasn't prepared to hear.

She hadn't attended the funeral, instead offering a feeble excuse about tight finances and the demands of her studies. But the real reason was harder to admit—she didn't know how to face it. The weight of unresolved emotions, the years of distance, the unspoken words—it was easier to turn away than to confront the finality of it all.

So, she withdrew, shutting her dad out, ignoring his calls, and burying herself in the relentless noise of a life already filled with hurt she hadn't begun to untangle. In the midst of it all, she built another reality—one where she was Lola, Brett was her anchor, and love once again became her refuge.

The silence between them now was heavy, though not uncomfortable. Her father sighed deeply, absently brushing a fallen leaf from the bench beside him. Hannah traced the edge of her jacket sleeve with her thumb, her eyes fixed on the river ahead.

The water shimmered in the afternoon light, rippling gently like the memories she tried to keep at bay.

Around them, the soft rustle of trees and distant birdsong filled the air. They sat side by side, each lost in their thoughts yet tethered by the quiet ache of shared pain and the unspoken weight of lingering sorrows.

Chapter Thirty: Sheena, Lola, Hannah

After what felt like a very long moment of silence, her dad said, "Sheena was the name your mum gave you after you were born. She liked the name and insisted you have an Irish name, too," Tom said softly, his voice barely masking the heaviness in his heart.

"I know," Hannah replied, a faint wry smile crossing her tear-streaked face.

There was a pause before Tom spoke, his voice soft and concerned. "So, how does it work with you and... the others?"

Hannah lowered her gaze, twisting her fingers nervously. "I'm still trying to figure it out. After the termination, something inside me broke. I felt shattered—and then, a part of me stepped in to hold everything together."

She took a breath before continuing. "Sheena has always been there, the fearless side ready to take over when things get overwhelming. In a way, she was the one who pushed me to come to Australia—I wanted to escape the pain and start anew. For a while, I even thought I could manage without her."

Her voice softened as she recalled another memory. "Then, when Christina was born, Lola emerged—the nurturer determined to make life work, no matter the struggle. Sometimes, they feel so real, like separate people with distinct voices. They even disagree with each other about what we remember."

Tom's eyes searched hers. "Does that mean you ever feel like you're not in control?"

Hannah paused. "Yes, there are moments when I feel like I'm just an observer, watching from the sidelines. It's confusing, but I'm learning to accept that these parts—Sheena, Lola, and the rest—are all pieces of who I am."

She paused, her breath catching in her throat as memories washed over her. She cast her mind back to when she had found out she was pregnant with

Chrissie. It had started with the sharp pang of nausea on that road trip to South Australia.

The crisp, early morning light in Adelaide when she'd woken up feeling unwell. The bitterness of coffee turning her stomach. She had chalked it up to exhaustion from travelling, but deep down, she had known.

"It was terrifying when I found out I was pregnant," Hannah whispered. "It felt like France all over again, like I was reliving that nightmare. I finally told Brett, and he was so supportive and understanding, but I couldn't shake the fear." She said, shaking her head slowly.

"That's when Lola slowly emerged—optimistic, nurturing, determined to make it all work – a bit like *Grandma Nigeria*. She made me believe we could do this together. And for a while, it worked."

Tom nodded, his face etched with sorrow as he listened.

"When Brett's parents insisted we move in with them after Chrissie was born, Lola felt assured that it would be okay." Hannah's voice was steady, but there was an undercurrent of something darker beneath it.

"Sheena, though... Sheena hated it," she continued, her expression tightening. "Living under their roof, it felt like I was suffocating. Brett seemed to shrink into himself, becoming this timid version of the man I fell in love with."

She let out a sharp breath, shaking her head. "His dad, Gareth, was already unwell, but he was so stubborn, so set in his ways. He refused to acknowledge how sick he was. And he had this... this way of making everyone feel on edge."

Hannah's fingers curled unconsciously, recalling the way Gareth used to pull everyone's strings back then—controlling, manipulating, holding onto his authority even as his body betrayed him.

"After Christina was born, things got worse. Gareth adored Chrissie, but he used his illness as leverage to keep us there longer. It was suffocating. I wanted out, but I understood Brett's dilemma - or at least Lola did. Sheena, though? Sheena was furious, and she was starting to take over."

Hannah's voice broke, her hands trembling. "And then... it happened," she said, her words barely above a whisper. Her lips quivered as she tried to continue, but the memory was too painful.

Tom exhaled; his breath unsteady. He had only met Chrissie once—just after she was born when she was about six months old.

He and Abi had flown to Melbourne then, full of excitement, cradling their granddaughter in their arms for the first time, never imagining it would also be the last.

They had thought there would be more time, more visits. They had made plans to visit more, looking forward to seeing her again and watching her grow. But instead... Regret settled deep in his chest, heavy and immovable.

He reached out and pulled Hannah into his arms, his embrace firm yet tender. "It's okay, Hannah. You don't have to say it," he murmured, though his voice was thick with grief.

But the memories came rushing back anyway.

Chapter Thirty-One: The Forgotten Day – November 2011

That morning, Gareth had insisted on a beach outing. Hannah had refused, exhaustion from sleepless nights with Chrissie weighing heavily on her.

"Why do we even need to go?" she'd snapped at Brett, her irritation spilling over.

"He thinks it'll be a nice family day out," Brett had replied, his voice apologetic.

She exhaled sharply, shaking her head. "Well, maybe it's time you tell them the truth—that we've started looking for a place. That *we*—me, you, and Chrissie—need our own space. We need to start building our life together as a family. It's not normal staying with them this long. It's suffocating, Brett. I don't like it. I need my own space. *Our* privacy."

Brett, avoiding her gaze, had said. "I'll talk to them," but there was little conviction in his voice. "Maybe later tonight."

Hannah had scoffed but said nothing more, retreating to their room to catch up on sleep. She had relished the quiet once they left, a rare reprieve from the constant noise of Gareth's commentary and the demands of motherhood.

The shrill ring of her phone shattered the peace.

"Hannah, it's me. Hann - you—I—oh God. Oh my God, I -" Brett's voice was frantic, breathless.

Her heart raced. "What? Brett, slow down. What's - what's happening?"

"It's Chrissie. Oh God, Hannah, Ah! No - no - no! she—she's drowned – I -." His words came in broken sobs.

The phone slipped from her hand, clattering to the floor. A sharp jolt of shock coursed through her, her mind screaming in denial even as her body moved on autopilot. She grabbed her keys and stumbled to the car; her vision clouded by a haze of anguish.

The drive was a blur. She didn't exactly know where she was going. Her hands gripped the steering wheel so tightly that her knuckles hurt. She didn't even see the oncoming car until it was too late.

…———— ⚜ ————…

Hannah woke in the hospital to the low, constant hum from the machines. Brett sat beside her, his face haggard and pale, his eyes red from crying.

"Chrissie. It wasn't a dream, was it?" she whispered, her voice cracking.

Brett shook his head, his shoulders trembling. "Gareth… he had a stroke. He had gone a little further into the water with Chrissie. He was holding her, and he—he couldn't…" His voice broke, and he buried his face in his hands.

When the stroke had occurred, Gareth had lost his grip on his granddaughter. It had taken some minutes before someone had noticed what had happened. By then, it was too late for Chrissie.

Hannah's world shattered. "I never even kissed her goodbye," she wailed, her cries echoing through the sterile room.

The nurses rushed in, sedating her as her grief consumed her.

When she woke again, Sheena had taken over. Hannah receded into the depths of her fractured mind, unable to face the unbearable pain. Sheena would take care of everything now.

…———— ⚜ ————…

Tom held his daughter close, his embrace tightening as emotions swelled. His voice was filled with regret as he whispered, "I'm so sorry, Hannah. I wish I could have been there for you. I wish I could have done more."

"It's not your fault, Dad," Hannah said, her voice muffled against his shoulder. But deep down, she wondered if anyone—herself included—could ever truly be absolved.

The silence between them was heavy, but it carried the weight of understanding, shared pain and the fragile hope of healing.

146

Chapter Thirty-Two: Hello and Goodbye

The rain drizzled softly against the café window, blurring the city lights beyond the glass. Sheena wrapped her hands around the warmth of her coffee cup, her fingers tapping absently against the ceramic. Across from her, Alex sat in silence, his own cup untouched, his gaze heavy with something unspoken.

They had met here countless times before — in moments of transition when life seemed too complicated to unravel anywhere else. This time, though, there was no escaping what needed to be said.

"I wasn't sure you'd come," Alex admitted, his voice lower than usual.

Sheena smirked, though there was no humor in it. "You always knew I would."

A long pause settled between them, the kind that carried years of history. Sheena exhaled, her breath fogging slightly against the rim of her cup.

"So, this is it?" Alex asked.

Sheena leaned back in her chair. "I think it has to be."

His voice was steady, but his fingers curled tightly around the edge of the table. "I guess we have been walking in circles. Maybe it's time we stopped."

She nodded slowly, the weight of the moment settling over her. "I don't regret any of it, you know."

"Me neither." He looked at her then, really looked at her, as if memorizing her face one last time.

Sheena continued, "But we can't keep doing this. It's not fair— to Brett, Natasha, to me, to you."

Sheena let out a quiet laugh, shaking her head. "Funny. I always thought we were the ones meant to be."

Alex swallowed hard, his expression conflicted. "Maybe in another life."

Sheena hesitated before speaking again, the words catching in her throat. "Alex. I need to tell you something," she finally said, her voice softer now. "About why I disappeared... why I've been so back and forth with you."

Alex tilted his head slightly, watching her with that same patient curiosity he always had.

"I wasn't just running away from you, Alex. I was running from myself." Sheena's fingers tightened around her cup. "There are parts of me I didn't understand back then. Things I've only just started to figure out. I—I wasn't always Sheena. Sometimes I was someone else. And I didn't even know it was happening."

His brows furrowed, but he didn't interrupt.

"I've been in therapy," she admitted. "Trying to understand what's been happening in my mind, why I shut people out. It's not just you I pushed away... it was everyone."

Alex let out a slow breath, nodding slightly. "That... makes sense. I mean, I always knew something was going on, but I didn't know how to ask."

Sheena gave him a small, sad smile. "I wouldn't have known how to answer, anyway."

She paused, inhaling deeply before looking up at him again. "There's something else," she said, her voice quieter now. "Something I never told you."

Alex frowned slightly but remained silent, waiting.

"I had a child," she whispered, her voice barely above a breath. "Before we met."

Alex's eyes widened, surprise flickering across his face. Sheena took a deep breath, forcing herself to continue. "Her name was Chrissie. She was beautiful... and she was mine. And I lost her."

The words hung between them, raw and unfiltered. Sheena had never said them out loud like this before and had never let herself be this vulnerable with him.

Alex's expression softened, his fingers twitching as if he wanted to reach for her but wasn't sure if he should. "Sheena... I had no idea."

She nodded, blinking against the sting in her eyes. "I didn't know how to tell you. I didn't know how to carry it. So I ran."

A silence fell again, but this time, it felt final. Sheena reached for her bag, standing up slowly. "Take care of yourself, Alex."

"You too," he said, his voice barely above a whisper.

She hesitated for a moment before stepping away and walking toward the door. As she pushed it open, the bell above jingled softly, marking her exit. She didn't look back.

Outside, the rain had stopped, leaving behind the scent of damp pavement and something else—something new. Sheena inhaled deeply, then exhaled, letting the past go with it.

Chapter Thirty-Three: Letting Go

"So, you're sure you want to do this?" Brett asked softly as he watched Hannah carefully fold her clothes, tucking them into the travel bag on the bed.

She nodded, her movements deliberate. "I think it needs to be done, Brett. I never got to say a proper goodbye to my mum. I owe it to her and myself to find some closure."

As she zipped up the bag, her thoughts drifted to another visit—one she had put off for years. Chrissie's grave.

For the longest time, the idea of standing before that cold, etched stone had felt unbearable, like willingly reopening a wound that had never and would never fully heal. But she had gone.

Brett had been beside her, steady and unwavering. Her dad, too, had made the journey with her, his grief just as raw, just as heavy.

And when she had finally spoken about it in therapy, unravelling years of suppressed pain, it had been like loosening a knot that had kept her bound for so long.

She remembered kneeling before Chrissie's headstone, tracing the letters of her daughter's name as though touching them could bring back the warmth of her tiny hands.

"I don't know if you can hear me, sweetheart," she had whispered, her voice barely holding steady. "I don't know if you're close or if you're somewhere far, far away, where time doesn't move the way it does here." She said shakily.

"But I need you to know—I carried you with me, even when I couldn't bear to say your name out loud. I thought if I said it, I'd break apart. But you were always there, Chrissie. In the quiet, in the spaces between my thoughts. And I am so sorry I couldn't save you."

A tear slipped down her cheek. "I will always love you. Always. But I have to keep going now. I think... I think it's time."

She had placed a single daisy beside the headstone—the kind of flower Chrissie had once reached for with delight in their backyard.

Now, she needed to brace herself for a similar reckoning. Facing her mother's grave felt just as daunting. But running from it hadn't erased the ache or silenced the questions. She had made peace with Chrissie's memory. Maybe—just maybe—she could do the same with her mum.

The decision hadn't come easily. She'd spent half the night talking it through with her dad and Brett, weighing her fears against the need to move forward.

Returning to the UK after so long felt monumental, overwhelming even. But it was necessary.

"It'll be good to do some travelling too," she added after a pause. "And maybe even see Ona again."

Her father had raised an eyebrow when she mentioned Ona during their conversation.

"You mean you two still keep in touch? That's impressive! I thought you'd lost contact after we moved to France."

Hannah had smiled faintly, her mind drifting back to those early years when she and Ona exchanged letters and emails, snapshots of their lives bridging the distance.

She had confided in Ona about her first big crush, Antoine, and Ona had shared stories of her new life in America—how different it was from their school days in Nigeria.

But then, everything had gone wrong.

The incident with Antoine—the shame she had never wanted to face—had made her retreat into silence. She stopped replying to Ona's emails, ignored her calls, and let their friendship wither.

Years later, curiosity led her to search for Ona on social media. She found her—married, living in the U.S., raising two boys. Ona had built the life she had always dreamed of.

Hannah had hovered over the "Add Friend" button, debating whether to reach out. But how could she explain her absence? How could she face the hurt she had caused? The fear of pity, of judgment, had stopped her.

Instead, she imagined conversations with Ona, recorded voice notes she never sent, and confided in a version of her friend she had created.

Her dad's voice had broken the spell of her thoughts.

"I saw her mum a few years ago at a conference in Washington. It was purely by chance, but she was thrilled to see me. She asked about you, you know. She said Ona still wonders about you. She missed you."

The weight of guilt settled over Hannah like a heavy cloak.

A week had passed since her father's arrival, and the decision to leave Australia had been made. There was no turning back.

"It's just for a while," she murmured, folding a pair of culottes and tucking them into her travel bag.

Brett sat at the edge of the bed, his expression caught between relief and sorrow. "Will you be okay, though?" he asked quietly.

She turned to him, her light brown eyes soft and searching. "I think so."

A small smile flickered on her full lips, tinged with sadness. "I'll miss you. You know that, don't you?"

"What's new?" he teased, a wry smile tugging at his lips.

Hannah laughed quietly, though the sting between her eyes betrayed the emotions simmering beneath the surface. The dim light cast a warm glow on her amber skin, accentuating the curve of her cheekbones and the gentle slope of her button nose. Her thick curls framed her face, shifting slightly as she steadied herself. Then, without another word, she crossed the room and wrapped her arms around him, holding on as if memorizing the feel of him.

"I'll miss you too," she whispered. "But... I think we both deserve this. We deserve a chance to heal, to make peace with the past. To finally let go."

She sat beside him, hesitating before reaching for his hand. Her fingers trembled slightly. "Brett... I need to tell you something."

He stilled himself, waiting.

"When I thought I was pregnant recently, I panicked," she admitted, her fingers twisting together. "Thankfully, I wasn't—it was just stress messing with my cycle." She let out a nervous laugh, but it faded quickly.

She took a shaky breath before continuing. "But at the time—when I truly believed I might be—I was terrified. Everything I'd buried came rushing to the surface. All my fears, all my guilt. It was overwhelming."

Her voice wavered as she forced herself to go on. "I realized it wasn't something I wanted. The idea of being pregnant again, of losing another child... it was too much. So, I—well, Lola—started to question everything. About you. About us."

Brett listened intently, his jaw tightening.

"Sheena wanted me to confront it all, but in her own chaotic way. And in some ways, I'm more like her now than I ever thought I'd be. But I'm ready—ready to embrace all of myself. My traumas are part of my past, but they don't have to define me."

Brett said, his face etched with understanding and sorrow. "I've blamed myself for so much," he admitted. "For letting my dad control our lives. For losing Chrissie. For losing you. For... that godforsaken day." His voice faltered, gaze dropping to the floor.

"I thought... if I could just make it up to you somehow..." He swallowed hard. "Even when you were dissociating, pretending Chrissie was still with us, or when Sheena or Lola came through—I thought maybe that was my way of protecting you. I told my mum not to mention Chrissie and what had happened when she was around you." He let out a bitter chuckle.

"She noticed, though. She even asked if we were sure about getting back together after everything."

Hannah squeezed his hand. "You don't have to do that anymore, Brett," she said firmly. "And you have to stop blaming yourself."

A fierceness crept into her voice—one that felt more like Sheena than Lola or Hannah. "I want you to take a page out of Sheena's book. Do something bold. Stop putting everyone else first all the time. You deserve more than that."

Brett's eyes widened, startled. "Is that who you want to be now?" he asked. "Sheena?"

Hannah hesitated. "I don't know," she admitted. "There are moments now when I feel like... all three of them at once. And it's not as scary anymore. They each have parts of me—parts that I love and need."

Brett nodded slowly, the edges of understanding forming in his expression.

Hannah pressed on, her voice soft but urgent. "I know you want to take care of your mum. But she'll be fine. She has her sisters, people who love her. You don't have to carry it all on your own." She let the words settle before continuing.

"You need to do something for yourself. Stop living in the past. It's time we both did."

She paused momentarily before speaking again. "And I think you need to talk to your dad. Even if he can't respond, he's still here. You need to tell him everything—how much he hurt you, how you never felt adequate enough growing up. Let it out. Make peace with it, with him... and with yourself. Before it's too late."

She had never had that chance with her mother. Their last conversation had ended abruptly, a sharp goodbye over the phone. She had told herself there would be time. But there hadn't been. She carried that regret like an open wound. She didn't want that for Brett.

His voice was barely above a whisper. "Can you ever forgive me?" His gaze searched hers, raw and aching.

"For everything? I should have told you," He admitted, voice hoarse. "About Chrissie. About everything. I thought... I thought I was protecting you, but I was also protecting myself," he said, looking down, sadness etched on his face.

"I was afraid that if I forced you to face the truth too soon, I would lose you completely. And after everything I'd already lost, I wasn't ready for that."

Hannah's expression softened, but she remained silent, letting him continue.

"I don't know if you can ever forgive me for that," Brett said, shaking his head. "For letting you believe she was still alive. For playing along instead of helping you through it in an honest and real way."

He exhaled, running a hand through his hair. "The truth is... I didn't know how to deal with any of it. I was grieving, too. I was barely keeping myself together, and I thought if I could just hold onto you—any version of you—then maybe I wouldn't fall apart completely."

His voice wavered, the weight of unspoken regret settling between them.

His jaw clenched as he looked down. "But that wasn't fair to you. I should have helped you process it, not hidden it from you. And I hate myself for that."

Hannah reached for his hand, squeezing it gently. "You were hurting too, Brett. You were trying to survive. We both were."

He let out a breath he hadn't realized he was holding. "I just... I need you to know I never wanted to deceive you. I just didn't want to lose you. And maybe that makes me selfish, but it's the truth."

Hannah's heart clenched. "There's nothing to forgive," she said softly. "My world was already split long before you came into it."

She hesitated before pulling out the silver chain he had given her years ago. Dangling from it, nestled against the pendant, was the engagement ring he had once slipped onto her finger.

She traced the smooth metal with her thumb before holding it out to him. "I guess... you'll be needing this."

A silence stretched between them, thick with unspoken words.

Brett let out a quiet laugh, blinking back tears. "No," he murmured. "Keep it. How else would you remember me?"

Hannah inhaled deeply, then met his gaze.

"I don't need anything to remember you."

She reached for his hand once more. "Promise me you'll be okay, Brett, and that you'll take care of yourself. That maybe—just maybe—you'll finally chase your travel photography dream. Do more of those things you love."

He smiled, eyes glistening. "I promise," he whispered. "I'll do it. For you. For Chrissie."

…——— ⚜ ———…

A few days later, they stood at Tullamarine airport, the bustle of travellers and the crackling announcements forming a backdrop to their quiet goodbye.

Hannah and her dad had decided to travel to Europe together, starting in the UK and then visiting other places that held pieces of their past, before heading to Italy, where Tom and Martha lived.

Tom stood to the side, watching Brett and Hannah with a soft expression. He knew how much they had been through together, and he felt a deep gratitude toward Brett for the role he'd played in his daughter's life.

Brett turned to Tom and extended a hand. "Thank you," Tom said as he shook it firmly. "For taking care of her when I couldn't. For being there for her through all of this."

"It was never a burden," Brett replied. "She's strong—stronger than she realizes."

Hannah smiled softly at their exchange; her travel bag slung over her shoulder. "I'll miss you, Brett," she said quietly.

"I'll miss you too," he said, his voice steady despite the emotion flickering in his eyes. "But I think this trip is exactly what you need. Both of you."

Tom placed a hand on Hannah's shoulder, and she looked up at him with a mixture of affection and determination. "Ready, love?" he asked gently.

She nodded, her gaze flickering back to Brett one last time. "Take care of yourself, okay? No more putting everyone else first."

"I promise," Brett said with a small smile. "And you promise me the same."

"I will," she said, her voice firm. Giving him a surprising wink. Was this Sheena saying goodbye?

As Hannah and her dad walked toward the gate, Brett stood there, watching until they disappeared from sight. He felt a pang of sadness but also a glimmer of something he hadn't felt in a long time—hope; Hope that he would come out of all this ok.

Walking beside her father, Hannah felt a strange but welcome lightness settle over her. She glanced at him, their steps in sync, and felt grateful for the chance to rebuild their bond.

For the first time in a long time, she allowed herself to believe that moving forward wasn't just possible—it was already happening.

Epilogue

It was an overcast day with a damp chill, which seemed to beg for cozy blankets and a steaming cup of tea. The clouds hung low and heavy, casting the world in muted shades of grey.

She had barely slept again, her rest broken by the same dream that had plagued her nights for weeks now. The dream was shifting, growing sharper in its details, as if her subconscious was trying to show her something she hadn't yet understood.

In the dream, she always stood on the edge of a vast shoreline, the sea churning violently before her. A voice would call out—a voice she would know anywhere. This time, she saw her mum more clearly, her figure emerging from the mist. At first, it was Sheena's appearance, which slowly morphed into her mum's face - radiant, her smile gentle, comforting, and achingly familiar. She cradled a baby in her arms—Chrissie. The baby cooed, tiny hands reaching for her.

Just as she started to step closer, waves as tall as mountains rose behind them. The water surged forward, crashing over them. Chrissie's smile was the last thing she saw before everything went dark.

She woke every time to the same hollow ache in her chest, clutching her sheets as if they could anchor her to reality.

Her mum's grave had become a place of quiet reflection for her, though each visit carried its own weight, pressing down like the damp chill of an autumn morning.

The cemetery was nestled at the edge of town, a secluded space where time seemed to move slower. Weathered headstones jutted from the earth at odd angles, some softened by moss, others marked by the delicate wilt of forgotten flowers. The branches of a towering yew tree swayed gently overhead, its dark needles whispering secrets to the wind.

The first time she had come, her dad had been by her side. She remembered how his presence had steadied her, an anchor against the tide of grief that had threatened to pull her under.

The air had been thick with the scent of damp earth and cut grass, and the silence between them had spoken louder than words.

When she knelt by the grave, tracing the engraved letters of her mother's name with trembling fingers, the weight in her chest had been unbearable.

Her tears had fallen in uneven droplets onto the marble, her voice breaking as she tried to speak, to say anything that could fill the hollow ache inside her.

Her dad had placed a firm, reassuring hand on her shoulder. He hadn't rushed her, but when her breaths turned shallow; when the sobs came in gasps, he had gently guided her back to the car.

She had barely registered the crunch of gravel beneath their feet. Her mind was fogged with sorrow, and her legs were weak, as if she had left part of herself behind in that quiet, sacred place.

The second time was different. She'd gone alone, more composed, though the grief still lingered in the corners of her mind, waiting to resurface.

She had sat cross-legged in front of the tombstone, Lola and Sheena sitting silently beside her, their heads down in contemplative reflection. Their presence was grounding, though they said little. She focused on the good memories, letting them wash over her like a soothing balm. She even laughed, recalling the time her mum had tried to make pancakes but, in her hungover state, had mistakenly used corn flour instead of regular flour.

"I reckon you were well and truly off your game that morning, Mum," she murmured, a bittersweet smile tugging at her lips.

The last time she visited, she had come prepared. She carried a fresh bouquet of her mum's favourite flowers—delicate pink peonies, their soft petals still kissed with morning dew.

She also brought something special: a portrait of her mum she'd sketched on waterproof paper. It was a labour of love, each stroke of charcoal capturing the warmth in her mum's eyes and the strength in her smile. She placed it carefully beside the headstone, the flowers arranged neatly at its base.

Her time in the UK had stretched longer than planned. She wasn't yet sure if she would stay permanently, but her dad had encouraged her to take her time.

He had given her the keys to her mum's old apartment in Hendon, a place that now felt like a time capsule of memories.

"Stay as long as you want. Your mum wanted you to have the apartment. She thought about renting it out or selling, but she always held out hope that you would return and want somewhere to stay." he had said before leaving for Italy. "Take your time with it. Do you think you'd want to stay here? In the UK?"

She had hesitated, the weight of the question pressing down on her. "I think so. I'll reach out to some of my contacts in the art space. I can start selling my work again, online and at fairs like I used to. And I'm almost done with my PhD program. I've spoken with my supervisor and deferred my viva examination," She had said, shrugging.

Her dad nodded. "That's all you need to do, Hannah. Take it one step at a time."

Now, she was back in the space that her mum had once called home. The apartment was quiet, save for the occasional creak of the floorboards beneath her as she sifted through her mum's belongings.

The late afternoon light filtered weakly through the lace curtains, casting intricate patterns on the wooden floor. A faded box sat in front of her, its corners worn soft with age, labelled in her mum's neat handwriting: *Keepsakes.*

Inside, she found old greeting cards, pressed flowers tucked between the pages of diaries, and trinkets that seemed too random to mean much to anyone but her mum.

And then, nestled at the bottom, she spotted a book with a leather cover, the edges cracked and fraying with time. It didn't seem like much at first, just an ordinary old book.

She flipped it open, the scent of aged paper rising faintly in the air. A photograph slipped out from between the pages, fluttering to the ground like a fragile leaf.

Hannah leaned forward, picking it up carefully, her breath catching as she turned it over. It was a photo of a little girl, maybe five or six years old. Her eyes were wide and curious, and her small heart-shaped face was familiar in a way that sent a shiver down Hannah's spine. The more she studied the features, the stronger the unease curled in her stomach. She could have sworn it was her.

But when she flipped the photo over, her breath hitched. The name scrawled in faded ink wasn't hers.

Her fingers trembled as she traced the unfamiliar letters, a chill sweeping through her - *Grace*.

Hannah's pulse pounded in her ears. She knew about Lola. She knew about Sheena. The fractures in her memory, the pieces of herself she'd uncovered, had already shaken the foundation of everything she thought she knew.

But if this girl wasn't her—if this was someone else—then who had she been before?

Her hands shook as she flipped desperately through the book. At the back, near the final pages, she found something else. A child's scribbles, uneven and faint, whispering a truth she wasn't sure she was ready for:

"Grace says I shouldn't tell. She says it's our secret."

Hannah stared at the words, nausea curling in her gut. She looked back at the photograph, her breath shallow. The little girl—her mirror image—smiled back at her, frozen in time. But it wasn't her name written on the back.

If there was Grace, if there had been someone else—someone before Lola and Sheena—how many more had there been? How far back did this go?

The truth was somewhere in this apartment, buried among her mum's carefully tucked-away treasures. But this was no longer just about her mother's secrets.

This was about Hannah's past.

A past that had been splintering far longer than she ever realized.

And for the first time, she wasn't sure if she wanted to remember.

THE END

About the Author

Adela Tobin has loved storytelling for as long as she can remember, weaving words into worlds where emotions run deep and characters find the courage to reclaim themselves. Born and raised in Nigeria, she moved to Australia eighteen years ago, carrying with her a heart full of dreams and a longing for adventure.

Her writing is inspired by the resilience of women, the beauty of reinvention, and the quiet moments that shape us.

Whether through fiction or personal reflection, she delves into themes of love, loss, identity, and the strength it takes to start over.

With a deep fascination for psychology, she loves to explore human emotions' complexities, relationships' intricacies, and the unseen forces that drive our choices.

She is also the author of *Surviving and Thriving in a Foreign Land and Reclaimed: Stories of Strength, Loss, and Becoming.*

When she's not writing, Adela finds joy in the simple things—tending to her garden, immersing herself in art and cultural festivals, and indulging in crafts that spark creativity.

Above all, she cherishes time with her daughter, who reminds her daily of the beauty in growth, discovery, and the ever-evolving journey of life.